# LADIES OF THE CANYON

## Advance Praise for *Ladies of the Canyon*

"Rarely and not at all in recent memory have I encountered a debut novel as polished and powerful and sure-footed as Douglas Wood's *Ladies of the Canyon*. Filled with compelling and wild-at-heart characters, clear-eyed observations about life's precarious road and set against a world at once alluring and dangerous, this is a winner in every conceivable way."
—Rick Kogan, Chicago Tribune

"Not since Carrie Fisher's *Postcards from the Edge* has there been a sharper gaze into the toxic nature of child stardom and fame in Hollywood. *Ladies of the Canyon* is a riveting story of addiction among child stars idled by the dark side of Hollywood and human emotion. A whodunit with a nasty twist!"
—Robert W. Walker, *Dead on Instinct*

"A scathing and scary Hollywood tale packed with more twists, turns and switchbacks than a rainy night on Laurel Canyon Boulevard. If you really want to know whatever happened to Baby Jane, read this book."
—Vince Waldron, co-author with Ronnie Spector of *Be My Baby: How I survived Mascara, Miniskirts and Madness or My Life as a Fabulous Ronette*

"Suspenseful and chilling. Wood explores the dark side of Hollywood with equal parts horror and wit."
—Anthony Lawrence, writer, The Twilight Zone

"It didn't take long for the characters in Douglas Wood's *Ladies of the Canyon* to spring from his imagination into my reality. When I glance at TMZ or Access Hollywood, I catch myself hoping for a segment on Devon O'Keefe or Nikki Barnes, before remembering their lives of celebrity, second chances, and disturbingly fierce determination, are fictional. (One hopes!)"
—Joel Paley, Author & Lyricist of *Ruthless! The Musical*

# LADIES OF THE CANYON

## DOUGLAS WOOD

PROSPECTIVE PRESS
Winston-Salem

# P ROSPECTIVE P RESS LLC

1959 Peace Haven Rd, #246, Winston-Salem, NC 27106 U.S.A.

www.prospectivepress.com

Published in the United States of America by PROSPECTIVE PRESS LLC

 TRADEMARK

## LADIES OF THE CANYON

Cover and interior design by ARTE RAVE

© PROSPECTIVE PRESS LLC, 2020

ISBN 978-1-63516-000-0

ProP-F007

First PROSPECTIVE PRESS Hardcover edition

Printed in the United States of America

First printing, August, 2020

The text of this book was typeset in Garamond Pro

### PUBLISHER'S NOTE

*For Valerie*

# *PEARL*

# PROLOGUE

I locked the bathroom door but it don't seem to do any good. Frank's strong. He pounds and kicks the door until it bursts open and he comes barreling in.

"Oh, for God's sakes," he says, disgusted.

He bends over the tub full of bloody water, picks up one of my arms and looks it over. He sees the cut I made from the wrist all the way up to the inside of my elbow. He lays my arm back down. I can't seem to keep my eyes open. Probably losing consciousness.

Frank lightly slaps my face, then again, harder. I open my eyes.

"This is getting old, Pearl, real old," he says.

"Just let me die, for Chrissakes."

"Don't tempt me," he says, grabbing a towel from the rack and wrapping it around my arm. He lifts me out of the water and I start to cry 'cause I failed once again. Now I have to keep living with what I know, what I've done. What I haven't done.

# *DEVON*

# CHAPTER ONE

Celebrities are always telling you not to believe everything you read in the press, but in my case it's all true. Shoplifting. DUIs. Restraining orders. Community service. Interventions. Rehab. Rehab again.

Let's just say for a young woman of twenty-three, I've led a full life.

I'll spare you a rehash of all of the above because what's the point. If you want the gory details, you can always Google me. All that matters at this moment in time is that I'm sober. "One day at a time," as they say. But that's the thing about those twelve-step platitudes—and why I use them sincerely, without irony or apology—they really are grounded in truth. And today I'm all about truth.

I'm at a Sunday morning meeting and not just any meeting; I've been asked to share and it's my first time. The church basement is small and cave-like and I'm feeling a little clammy. The meeting leader has one of those craggy faces that looks like it would shatter into a million pieces if he smiled. But he doesn't smile. He just whispers into the mic in a voice so soft I almost don't realize he's said my name.

I make my way up to the podium and look out at about twenty-five people. It's a typical West Hollywood crowd—film industry types, hipsters, LGBTQ, young and old, but nobody as young as me, not even close. There's one middle-aged woman who looks familiar but I can't quite place her. She's beautiful, in a ravaged sort of way, and she's staring at me. I break from her gaze and begin speaking.

"My name is Devon, and I'm a drug addict and alcoholic."

"Hi, Devon," everyone responds.

I've decided to speak off the top of my head, no notes. I'll save the script reading for when I'm at work. This isn't a performance, it's real life.

"I've been sober for thirty-three days."

People clap and it feels awesome—even better than any applause I've gotten from the crew after a particularly good take.

"They say one of the best parts of recovery is getting your feelings back. And, of course, the worst part is getting your feelings back." There's some light laughter.

"I'd be lying if I didn't admit I'm scared. I just got out of rehab where they decided my mother has been enabling my addiction—that she's the reason I keep relapsing. Apparently, it's not healthy for me to continue to live with her."

I barely get the words out. Tears well up in my eyes and I bite the inside of my cheeks so I won't cry. I hate when people get up here and cry. I take a deep breath and regain my composure.

"Yesterday she went back to Wisconsin after the social workers suggested she have no contact with me for the next few months. I'll be on my own for the first time ever. My father's dead. Cirrhosis of the liver seven years ago, so yeah, it's in the genes."

I look into the audience and see that the woman who was staring at me is hanging on my every word. Her mouth is slightly open and a tear rolls down her cheek. She swipes it away with the back of her hand.

"Thankfully, I still have a job. They put my series on hiatus for a month and I start back tomorrow. I'm grateful to have this second chance. Dealing with fame is a bitch, but when I was in rehab I met people who suffered *real* problems—poverty, abuse, homelessness."

A guy in the back nods knowingly. He leans so far back in his metal chair I'm afraid he'll crash.

"They made me realize how privileged I've been and how I've wasted so many opportunities. I've hurt a lot of innocent people—friends, family, co-workers. Ex-boyfriends. So I'm counting on a higher power to get me through this tough period. A lot of people are depending on me and I can't let them down. More importantly, I can't let myself down."

I realize I need to wrap up, but I'm distracted by the staring lady. She's now full-out crying, not just a few tears, but actual sobbing. The tatted guy next to her shakes his head, irritated, but the woman on the other side of her tries to console her and hands her a Kleenex, which she takes and blows her nose into. When she's done, I get a better look at her face and it hits me who she is—Nikki Barnes, one of the most notorious child stars-gone-bad, more famous for her drug abuse and various tabloid exploits than her show-biz career. She gets up and rushes out of the room, clearly embarrassed by her emotional outburst. I'm a little rattled, not sure what it is I've said that's set her off. I continue with my speech.

"Thanks for listening to me. Recovery is a journey, not a destination, so I appreciate all the support from you, my fellow travelers." Oh, God, did I actually say that out loud? I can't believe I ended with something so trite. I smile sheepishly, but no one seems to care because they're applauding enthusiastically.

The speakers that follow tell their tales of hardship and suffering. A few have been in prison. One woman describes being date-raped when she was too drunk to fight back. Another numbly relates how she's been court-ordered to attend meetings. I'm sympathetic to her story until she gets to the part where she left her four-year-old in a hot car. The child survived but is brain damaged.

One speaker looks remarkably like my dad and it makes me wish my mom and I could've convinced him to go to a meeting. I regret he never got a chance to see my career take off—he would've been proud. He was a high school English teacher and it was he who got me interested in reading—books, plays, and poetry, everything from David Sedaris to O'Neill. He's also the one who encouraged me to audition for school plays. "Read this," he said, tossing me a copy of *The Crucible* one day while I was doing my homework.

"Let's see you put some of your teen angst on stage where it belongs, my little drama queen." Somehow he knew I had talent before I did. I was cast as Abigail and suddenly my recent break-up with one Robbie Jurgensen was no longer the end of the world as we know it. For the record, I did *not* give him a hand-job during *Toy Story 3* despite what he told every student at Bradford High. Robbie—who I hope goes by Robert these days—was my first "bad boy." There would be many to follow, the unfortunate result of having a dad who could be Atticus Finch one moment and Chris Brown the next.

The man who looks like my dad speaks lovingly about his family but in the next breath mentions he's lost them to his addiction. He doesn't even know where his grown daughter lives now. "I might be a grandpa for all I know," he says, rubbing his stubbled face.

As riveting as these speakers are, I can't help but be preoccupied. Why was Nikki Barnes sobbing while I was speaking? I get up and head for the lobby, hoping she's there.

She is—standing alone next to a drinking fountain, dabbing her eyes with Kleenex. When she sees me, she calls my name, "Devon!" like we're old friends or something.

The first thing that strikes me about her is how pale her skin is, like a vampire who's never seen the light of day. Her eyes are impossibly large and soulful, sad actually. She has great bone structure, with prominent cheekbones, or maybe it's just because her face is so gaunt. Her short spiky hair is obviously dyed black—very 1980s. In her skinny jeans, tie-dyed T-shirt, and Converse All-Stars she looks kind of waifish, if that's possible for someone who looks every bit her age. There are lines around her mouth, her forehead, and her deep-set eyes. But I like her lived-in face.

When I'm close enough, she throws her arms around me and gives me a big hug that she holds for an uncomfortably long time. She reeks of cigarettes and I have to choke back a cough. I can't tell for sure, but I think she's crying again. What is *with* this woman?

Nikki finally lets go of me then thrusts her arm forward to introduce herself—"Nikki Barnes."

We shake. "Actually, I know who you are."

"Yeah, well, my reputation tends to precede me," she says. "Once your twat's been splayed out all over TMZ, there's no turning back."

I laugh. "No, no—I grew up watching reruns of *One More Thyme* on Nick at Night. I loved that show."

"You're sweet," she says, shoving her Kleenex in the pocket of her jeans. She looks down at the linoleum floor, as if she's embarrassed, then back up at me.

"Listen, I'm sorry for blubbering like an idiot in there, but your speech really touched me."

"Thank you," I say just as people start streaming into the lobby from the meeting room. Many of them are already reaching for their cigarettes.

"Would you like to grab some coffee?" Nikki asks.

This takes me by surprise. "Um, I'd love to but I'm sort of under the gun. I need to..." I'm not sure how much I want to tell this virtual stranger. "It's a long story," I say, hoping she'll let it drop. She doesn't.

"What? You can tell me."

I sigh. "I'm being evicted. Can't pay my rent at the Oakwood—that's where my mom and I were staying before she moved back to Kenosha. I blew through all my money on you-know-what so I need to find a cheap place to live. By tomorrow. Or I'm out on the street. Pretty pitiful, huh?"

"Small potatoes, babe. My own mother planted coke on me just to get me out of her house and into jail. 'Course it was sort of redundant since I was already carrying a fuckin' kilo of heroin." She laughs a throaty laugh that turns into a smoker's cough.

"So where 'ya headed?" she asks.

"The west valley. I have a 2:30 appointment to see a studio apartment in..." I pull out my phone, start scrolling. "...Chatsworth. I'm still not familiar with anything but the west side. Is that far from here?"

"Trust me. You don't want to live in Chatsworth."

"Oh. It's one of the few places I can afford. That, and a place in..." I scroll through my phone. "South Central?"

Nikki cracks up, starts coughing again.

"Devon, listen. You can stay with me until you get back on your feet. I live in Laurel Canyon. It's not luxurious, but you can have your own room. I've got tons of space."

I remind myself I just met this person two seconds ago. I also remind myself that I'm desperate. And someone told me Chatsworth is the porn capital of the world.

"Are you sure it's okay?" I ask. "You hardly know me."

"Of course I know you. You're *me*, thirty years ago!"

That explains the crying, I think. She heads for the double doors, apparently deciding the conversation's over. I follow her outside where she cuts through the cluster of smokers. Enveloped by haze, she looks like an apparition.

• • •

I'm driving into Laurel Canyon in my Mini Cooper, breathing in the scents of chaparral, sage, and eucalyptus, my new friend Nikki Barnes in the passenger seat. She told me she hitched to the meeting; her car's in the shop.

Sometimes my mom and I would take this canyon through the Hollywood hills to get to our furnished apartment at the Oakwood near Universal Studios. She found the canyon charming, appreciating the narrow, winding streets that reminded her of Europe. I'd never been to Europe, but I liked Laurel Canyon because lots of musicians and artists lived in its wooded hills and it had a funky country store at its center where I'd buy Snapple and Mint Milanos.

It's just minutes from the congested Sunset Strip, but you really feel like you're in a small, rural town when you're up here. When we first came to L.A., we used to fantasize that someday I'd be making enough money to live in this idyllic oasis of nature. My mom would ape Joni Mitchell's high voice and sing about the hippie chicks who lived here back in 1970—Trinna and Annie and Estrella, the "Ladies of the Canyon," who would bake and sew and sing and draw. I'd picture myself as one of those lovely canyon ladies but in my fantasy, there was always a hot canyon guy nearby, one of those long-haired types with wiry arms who made his own musical instruments out of trees.

"Turn left here, then follow this road all the way to the top," Nikki says, and we drive higher into the hills, past quaint cottages with peace sign flags, that sit next to multi-million dollar mansions with avant-garde sculptures in front.

"Once I start work I'll have plenty of cash coming in. I've got to pay off some debts," I explain, "but I'll be able to give you rent in a few weeks. And then, in a few more I should have enough to get my own place."

"Don't worry about it. You can stay as long as you like. It'll be good for me to have some company again. I've lived alone for I don't know how many years and that shit's getting old."

Nikki points up ahead. "See all that purple bougainvillea that's covering the carport? Pull in there."

I come to a stop behind a filthy yellow Porsche with four flat tires that looks like it's been sitting there a long time. I wonder if this is Nikki's other car, the one that's not in the shop.

"You don't have to pay a cent. I paid cash for this house years ago, so I only have utilities and property taxes to worry about...thank God for residuals."

The house is a two-story Spanish Colonial, enveloped by more bougainvillea and climbing vines. The stucco badly needs painting and some of the red terra-cotta tiles are missing, but the 1920s architecture is impressive and I feel like I've hit the jackpot. This is the kind of house I might've bought had I not squandered away my money on drugs.

"Here—take a look," Nikki says as she leads me through an archway on the driveway. Before us is a spectacular view of the canyon. Tall cypress trees in one direction, palm trees in another. Cabins and cottages dot the rolling hills like in a fairy tale. We come to the front entranceway. Nikki steps over a mound of junk mail and unlocks the door.

"This is so generous of you," I say. Nikki opens the door and we step inside. My smile instantly fades and my first thought is *what the hell have I gotten myself into?*

Any charm the Spanish-style interior might have—walls with rounded corners, wrought-iron bannisters, exposed wood beams—is obliterated by the worst of 1980s décor. It's as if Nikki purchased and decorated the mansion at the height of her fame and then just let the whole place deteriorate around her, never updating the furnishings or even maintaining them. I'm reminded of Miss Havisham in *Great Expectations*—the reclusive woman who suffered a mental breakdown when she was jilted by her fiancé and never left her crumbling manor.

The living room is so dark I have to squint; mangled vertical blinds, in mauve, no less, cover the windows and sliding doors, and I wonder why anyone would block out the breathtaking canyon view.

Nikki notices me scanning the room. She lights up a cigarette and says, "Take a look around," clearly proud of her not-so-humble abode.

The room is huge. One wall has peeling shiny pink and black vinyl wallpaper, another displays mirrors in geometric shapes. There's a wonderful fireplace but the space where logs should be is crammed with *Interview* magazines. Directly above it is an original Andy Warhol of Nikki, her unmistakable Margaret Keane eyes in impossibly vivid colors. Surrounding it are three framed posters bearing the signature "Nagel" depicting soulless New Wave women—jet black hair, porcelain skin, full lips.

In the center of the room are massive leather couches and chairs, ripped beyond compare. There's a pseudo Art Deco entertainment center the size of Milwaukee next to a hulking Pac-Man arcade video machine.

A wet bar is in one corner—dirty cocktail glasses and empty bottles evidence of a party that might've taken place last night or years ago. The lighting fixtures are garish monstrosities of brass and glass. The ceiling has brown water stains; soggy clumps of it litter the soiled wall-to-wall teal carpeting.

"Excuse the mess," Nikki says casually. "My maid's been sick for a few weeks so the place has gotten a little cluttered."

"No, no, it's fine," I say, trying to pretend the overpowering smell of mildew doesn't bother me. I glance down at my phone, the address of the Chatsworth apartment still on my screen. Surely not everyone who lives there is in porn, I tell myself. One night. Just one night at Nikki's. Tomorrow I'll scour L.A. for a place to stay. Doesn't matter how small it is, or if it has hardwood floors or gets southern exposure—it just has to be clean.

"Here, let me show you your room." Nikki leads me through the living room—we step over take-out containers and pizza boxes to a staircase that climbs up to the large second floor. Some of the Spanish tile risers are beautiful, others broken. We walk down the hallway past several rooms until we reach the last one. Nikki opens the door and we step inside a surprisingly large room.

"This used to be my office."

The first thing I notice is a faded cardboard standee of Nikki as her character Jennifer Thyme, smiling in the corner like a ghost. Yellowed Jennifer Thyme posters line the walls. Lots of cleavage and bare midriff, obviously made to appeal to testosterone-filled teenaged boys, or more likely, horny middle-aged men. There are two file cabinets and boxes of *One More Thyme* memorabilia stacked against the wall and on a desk.

"I used to have a staff to answer fan mail, send out autographs and shit. Long time ago."

I nod.

"The couch turns into a bed—it's pretty comfortable." She picks up a Cabbage Patch doll resting there and holds it in her arms as if it were a real baby. She speaks with the cigarette between her lips. "And there's an adjoining bathroom. That TV works too."

"Cool," I say and glance at the bulky dinosaur on a rolling stand. The only televisions I've seen like this are at the back of thrift shops or in old movies.

"Don't worry," she says, motioning toward all the boxes. "We can move all this crap into the garage."

Damn. I have to say something. I can't let Nikki go through all the trouble of cleaning up this room only to walk out on her tomorrow.

"Nikki—I don't know if this is such a good fit."

She looks at me and cocks her head as if she's having trouble hearing what I'm saying.

I search for words that won't sound harsh but can't find any. "We just... I think we may not be compatible exactly." Nikki doesn't say anything, just looks at me with deep concern, waiting for me to say my piece. I wuss out and place the blame on myself. "I'm sort of a neat freak," I lie.

"Got it!" she says, letting out one of her throaty laughs. "In my house, people wipe their feet on the way *out!* I'm a fucking *pig*—why didn't you just say so?"

Now she's got me laughing. "In Kenosha, we're told not to say such things, *aloud*, anyway. It would just be rude, or mean."

"At Casa Nikki it's just honest. I'm an open book, Devon. You can say just about anything to me without hurting my feelings. I've been dragged through the mud so many times, my skin is as thick as a crocodile's."

"Crocodile or pig," I ask. "Which is it?"

"Both." Nikki sits down on the lumpy couch. I remain standing, afraid if I sit down, I'll arise with an STD.

"I'm just now pulling out of a clinical depression. That's why my place looks so messy. That, and I don't have any cash to renovate it the way I'd like." Nikki looks down at the couch and smoothes her hand over the nubby fabric. When she looks up again, her face is that of an ashamed child.

"Do you know what it's like? To be depressed?" she asks, tentatively.

"Yes. Yes I do." And in that instant I decide to stay. Not sure for how long—a week, a month, however long it takes to get back on my feet. "I can help you clean. I'm really good at it. I spent one summer as a maid at the Value Inn." Cleaning gives me a sense of accomplishment. There's a beginning, a process, and a positive result. Kind of like getting sober.

"Then you'll stay? I could sure use the company."

"Of course," I say as a wave of sorrow sweeps over me. I don't know if it's for Nikki and her sad life or for me and mine. Maybe both. I feel the urge for a drug, any drug, and am glad I have nothing on me. *One day at a time*, I remind myself. I place my trust in the twisted higher power that has, for some strange reason, delegated washed-up Nikki Barnes as my savior.

# CHAPTER TWO

It's late Sunday afternoon, and a van arrives carrying everything in the world I own, which isn't much. Clothes, books, rugs, a comforter, some chotchkes. The van and its driver, Kyle, a young production assistant, are courtesy of my streaming TV series, *Beverly Hills Banshee*. Kyle's boxed up everything in my apartment and driven it over here.

I introduce him to Nikki.

"Whoa!" he says. "It's Jennifer Thyme!" If that weren't uncool enough, he starts singing the theme song to *One More Thyme*. And the dude is totally tone-deaf. Nikki handles it like a pro, dead-panning, "Please stop or I'll have to kill you."

I rush over to the van's passenger seat and find the carrying case holding my most valuable possession—Wheezer, my cat and bff. I pull him out, cuddle him, and speak in that ridiculous baby voice people use with their pets. I love this little gray furball; he's stuck with me through thick and thin. When I was in rehab, I missed him more than anybody, even my mom. And I worried that she wouldn't give him the kind of care and attention he needed. Nikki comes over and I transfer him into her arms.

"His name's Wheezer."

"Ooh, a Persian! Look at that little smashed-in face! Yep, he's wheezing all right. Oh, and he's *purring!*" Nikki looks up at me. "Does that mean he likes me?" There's something so childlike and vulnerable about the way she says this that my heart breaks a little.

"Yeah, Nikki, he likes you." I start to help Kyle unload boxes from the van. Nikki stands there for a moment longer, gently rubbing noses with Wheezer. I set down the heavy box I'm holding and take a picture of the two of them. It's an image that feels significant—sort of a symbol of my old life joining my new one. Nikki knows just how to handle Wheezer. She scratches him under the chin with her free hand, just the way he likes, erasing any doubts I may have had about sharing this perverse mansion with a fellow junkie. I remind myself that everything we judge in others is something within ourselves we don't want to face. It's not Nikki I need to worry about, it's me.

• • •

After we've unloaded the last of my stuff, Nikki checks the van to make sure it's empty.

"That's everything," she says, then furrows her brow and sniffs the air. She turns around to see Kyle exhaling a plume of smoke. He's holding a vape pen in his hand. He takes another hit and holds it out to her, grinning.

"All work and no play..." he says.

Nikki grabs the vape from his hand and hurls it into the grassy hills. She gets in his face. "Out!"

"What the fuck!" says Kyle.

"Oh, my god, Nikki. I had no idea..." I say.

Nikki gives Kyle a big shove. "Now! Get the fuck outta here!" For someone so skinny, she's pretty strong.

"Geez, it's only weed," Kyle says. "What—you tryna' tell me you don't party?"

Nikki starts beating on Kyle with her balled-up fists. And not lightly—she's really pounding the crap out of him, landing punches on his arm, his shoulder.

"Ow! That hurts!"

"She just came out of rehab, you tool! Use your brain!" she says, slapping him on the head, dismantling his sadly outdated man bun.

"Sorry, I didn't think a little pot was any big deal," Kyle says as he scurries into his van.

He looks at me. "See you tomorrow at work?" he asks in a weak high voice that almost makes me laugh. I just stare at him as he drives off, one hand on the wheel, the other soothing his bruised shoulder.

"Man!" says Nikki. "Can you believe him? That's the *last* thing you need right now. Assholes like that hanging around."

"You're right. I swear, I don't know what I would've done if you hadn't been here." Actually, I *do* know. I throw my arms around Nikki and give her a hug.

"Thank you," I say and before you know it, I'm the one crying. Nikki doesn't say anything, just strokes my hair.

• • •

Wheezer and I are curled up together on my open sofa bed in my new digs. The room actually looks pretty decent now—Nikki and I moved a lot of junk into her garage and I scoured the place from top to bottom. I covered the dingy carpet with a kilim rug and lit some scented candles to help cover up the musty odor. With my books and photos around me, it's starting to feel kind of homey. The window's open and I can hear owls hooting. It's a comforting sound—I used to hear them at Petrifying Springs Park, my favorite place to hike back home in Kenosha.

When I was wiping down the DVD player I found a disc underneath labeled, "Where Are They Now?" which I just watched. It's a segment that aired a few years ago on the E! channel and while it was a good way to get to know my new roomie, it's left me feeling unnerved. I was hoping to get to bed early since tomorrow's my first day back at work, but now I'm on edge. The Nikki Barnes tale is definitely not a cheery bedtime story.

Like me, Nikki became a household name almost overnight when she landed the title role in a TV series. *One More Thyme* was a sitcom that dealt with fifty-five year-old parents, the Thyme's, trying their best to raise their unplanned daughter, Jennifer, now a "New Wave" teenager. It was the "Don't Worry, Be Happy!" Reagan-era, and fluff like this was really popular. You know the kind of show—broad acting, lots of one-liners and loud laugh tracks.

The nation watched Nikki grow up *literally* in front of its eyes. By the time the series ended, after a successful five-year run, Nikki had blossomed from a baby-faced adolescent into a major babe.

That's when the trouble started. Like so many former child stars, she really had no training and developed bad acting habits on the sitcom. No one in the industry would take her seriously, so she started abusing alcohol and drugs. She was forced to take the only jobs being offered— starring roles in teen sexploitation pictures like *Hollywood High Hustlers,* or bottom-of-the-barrel slasher flicks.

It was on the set of *Groupie Ghouls from Hell* that she met rock star T.J. Colton, bad-boy lead singer for the heavy-metal band Moist. After a three-week courtship they got married and then, to no one's surprise, divorced just two months later.

Nikki gave birth shortly after the split to a baby girl, Julia, who was born with a rare congenital respiratory disease. Nikki put her career on hold and devoted her life to her daughter. She became a spokeswoman for the disease and was a familiar sight on Oprah and all the afternoon talk shows, trying to raise money for research.

But her efforts were in vain: Julia died on her fourth birthday. Nikki wrote a best-selling memoir about her devastating period of mourning and did the afternoon talk show circuit again. Her ex-husband, on the other hand, couldn't overcome the tragedy—T.J. died two months later of a drug overdose. It was never determined if it was suicide or not.

Nikki made a few regrettable made-for-TV movies in the years that followed, usually a disease-of-the-week drama, but her face was seen more frequently on the front page of the tabloids. Check out these headlines— it's like all the reporters went to the same bad school of journalism:

THYME TO PURGE – BARNES ADMITS 'I'M BULIMIC!'
JAIL THYME FOR SHOPLIFTING!
DUI ONE MORE THYME!
EX SITCOM LOLITA BARES ALL IN HUSTLER!
THYME FOR REHAB – NIKKI BARNES TO BETTY FORD!

In the years that followed, Nikki was caught up in the vicious cycle of addiction and recovery that I've also experienced, punctuated by a few failed career comebacks.

She blew most of her savings on drugs and legal fees.

The segment ends with Nikki declaring she's living a clean and sober life in her Laurel Canyon mansion. While she insists she has no desire to return to a sitcom, she expresses interest in hosting a talk show that would explore topics important to her, such as at-risk youth.

I've turned out the lights but each time I close my eyes I see images of the emaciated face of Nikki's daughter Julia and a tiny casket being lowered into the ground. I squeeze Wheezer and give him a bunch of kisses; he curls up against my chin. Eventually, I calm down, and his purring is the last thing I hear before finally drifting off to sleep.

• • •

A huge "Welcome Back, Devon!" banner decorates the soundstage. Each person I pass stops to give me a hug— everyone from the grips to my co-stars. A lighting guy who I know only as Levon hugs me so hard I fear my ribs will break. It's awkward as hell because after the hug neither of us knows quite what to say. Thankfully, another hugger comes by, Pat, the make-up artist.

"It's great to have you back!" she says, which carries the subtext, *please don't relapse, bitch, I really need this job.* The last time I saw these kind, hardworking people I was strung out on cocaine, two hours late for rehearsal and struggling to remember my lines. I want to apologize to each colleague individually, but it would be unprofessional to bring that kind of baggage into work right now and besides, making amends is steps eight and nine and I'm not there yet. The feeling of shame overpowers me and of course, my first thought is to get high to avoid feeling. Instead, I head over to the craft services table and grab a donut, one of the few vices left on my "okay" list. I bite into an obscene chocolate custard, one that almost convinces me I don't need drugs after all.

It's time for the table read. The mood is generally lighthearted and everyone laughs a little too hard at the few lame jokes, or offers an occasional "aw" at the poignant moments to make the writers feel good. If something bombs or sounds awkward coming out of the actors' mouths, the writers make notes and later return to the writers' room to make revisions.

One of the producers, Dan Jacobson, starts out by welcoming me back to the show. Everyone applauds and there are even a few whistles by the crew. All eyes are on me and I think I'm expected to make some sort of speech, but all I'm capable of is a quick, "Thanks, everyone. It's good to be back." After all the drama I've created and the bad behavior I've displayed, the less said the better.

The table read goes well and afterwards I get another hug-fest. The last hug is with Dan, who whispers, "My office," into my ear. I follow him in and he tells me to close the door. I'm not too intimidated—Dan's a laid-back kind of producer, a jeans and gym shoes kind of guy, and sure enough, he puts his legs up on his desk, and starts eating take-out sushi with chopsticks. So I'm thinking, how serious can this meeting be?

"Okay, kiddo," he says with his mouth full. "These are the rules: You show up on time, not a minute later. You come to rehearsals knowing your lines. You take breaks with everyone else—no sneaking off to your dressing room every few minutes. You still with me?"

"Uh-huh."

"No surprises with your appearance." He puts down his chopsticks and holds out one of his hands, using his fingers to count. "That means no far-out haircuts, no weight loss, no scars on your arms." He stops to eat more sushi and I'm relieved he didn't have to use his other hand. But this is much worse than I expected. He's as harsh as my old gym teacher, Coach Amundsen, who once called me a brat just because I forgot my uniform.

"Geez, Dan. Could you *be* any more humiliating?"

"I'm not done. You go to meetings daily. They're right here on the lot so there's no excuse. You tinkle in a jar for us everyday."

"Tinkle. Absolutely."

"And stay out of the limelight. You get busted for anything, I don't care what—shoplifting, baring your tits in public, jaywalking, you're off the series. Kira Franklin's a beautiful and talented supporting actress and I'm sure she'd love to be bumped up, aren't you?" he says. He gestures with his chopsticks toward nothing in particular.

"Of course."

"Any questions?"

"Yes, are you going to finish your spicy tuna roll?" When feeling ambushed, I aim for levity.

He smiles. "It's yours," he says, and passes me the sushi.

"Thanks, Danny," I say quietly and he knows I'm referring to way more than the tuna.

"Tough love, kiddo. If I didn't care about you, you wouldn't be here."

"I know that." I pop the piece of sushi into my mouth and for a moment there's no sound except our mutual chewing.

"Not bad, huh?" Danny asks.

"Um," I say, my mouth full of rice.

"So, I heard about your mom moving back home. That's good. You two were way too close. Where you living now?"

"I'm staying at a friend's house." He raises his eyebrows like he wants to know more.

"A new friend," I add. "Nikki Barnes."

He lifts his legs off the desk and leans forward. *"Are you shitting me?"*

"I know she's a little... bizarre, but—"

"*Bizarre?* She's a fuckin' junkie!" He grabs his bottle of water, squeezes it, and downs some, like an athlete after a game.

"No, she's not. She's been sober for like... I don't know, a while now. And she's been really sweet to me."

"Look—we both know if you don't want to slip, you stay away from slippery places."

"Please, Danny. I'm asking you not to judge her. I think she's a good person."

He looks unconvinced. He picks up a piece of sushi with his chopsticks, but he doesn't eat it. Instead, he just tosses it back down in the plastic container.

"And it's only temporary," I say. "When I start making some money again, I'll get my own place."

"I can't tell you what to do, but I gotta be honest with you—your judgment concerns me. We're taking a big risk letting you back on the show again. There are many people whose livelihoods are at stake and times are tough."

I take this in. The thing is—for a twenty-three year old I've made few life decisions by myself—my mother usually made them for me. And, of course, many of her decisions turned out to be destructive. Like procuring drugs for me and letting me use in the apartment. She felt it was safer than my scoring questionable dope on the streets and turning on with god-knows-who. Maybe she was right. I guess we all aspire to make the right choices, but sometimes things aren't so clear-cut.

"Devon? Have you heard what I've said?" I look up and realize I've been in my head.

"Yes, I have." We stare at each other and I realize all traces of the "nice Dan" are gone; all that's left is hostility. I feel like I'm in an improv that's going nowhere fast; we're no longer connecting, just sharing the same space. I decide to initiate a new beat and see where it goes.

"What if I bring Nikki to rehearsal tomorrow so you can meet her yourself, get your own sense of her?"

Dan lets out a sigh, then nods his head. It's like he can't even muster up the energy to spit out a word. Our bad improv is over. There's not much I can do, so I slip out quietly, mumbling, "See you tomorrow." He doesn't respond.

• • •

By the time I bring home Chinese chicken salads from Chin Chin, it's about 9:00 PM. Nikki and I hang out on the back deck off her bedroom, sipping chamomile tea. The canyon is storybook beautiful at night; the lights of nearby cottages twinkle and the pungent smell of night-blooming jasmine is our only intoxication. I can see into the yard next door where a sixtyish Asian man sits nestled in a stone grotto area. An old school CD player plays primitive music that sounds like bamboo flutes, and for a moment I feel like I'm in Tibet. I'm more relaxed than I've been in a long time—it's like the canyon itself has put me under its spell.

"That's Andy Chiu, meditating. Every night at 9:00 he's out there, like clockwork. You know him?" Nikki asks.

"I think so. Isn't he like a 'healer to the stars?'"

Nikki nods. "He knows the whole history of this canyon. Well, maybe not the *whole* history—but everything from the sixties on. Janis Joplin lived here. Mama Cass, Jim Morrison. Dead, dead, and dead. The Houdini mansion used to be over that hill." She points in the distance. "But nobody's ever proved he really lived there. Kids still show up every Halloween, though, and have séances and shit."

"Cool."

"Manson lived here too, with a bunch of hippies in some caves built for a movie set. That was only a few years before the Sharon Tate massacre—you've heard of her?"

"Yeah, Margot Robbie played her in *Once Upon a Time in Hollywood.*"

Nikki laughs. "Yeah, only in real life the chick was stabbed sixteen times."

"But in the movie she lives. Brad Pitt and Leonardo DiCaprio kill the Manson family gang."

"And everyone lived happily ever after. Big difference between movies and reality, my friend." Nikki lights a cigarette and continues. "The Wonderland murders weren't too far from here. You know, the whole thing with... what's his name... the guy with the dick."

I have no idea what she's talking about. I make a mental note to Google this stuff later.

"My memory's for shit. Holmes. John Holmes. The porn star." She takes a drag on her cigarette. "Yep," she says, imitating a grizzled old man, the kind who cryptically warns teenagers of danger in every grade-Z horror movie ever made. "You be careful now, 'ya hear? Reckon there's a lot of crazy stuff happenin' in these here hills, if'n you get my drift."

"I get your drift, mister," I say playing along. We each take in the night, the crickets.

"Hey," Nikki says in another of her voices, this one vaguely mafioso. "I'm the one who's doin' most of the yakkin' heah." She looks at me with a concerned face. "What gives?"

"I'm just... I don't know... scared."

"What's scaring you, sweetie? My creepy stories?"

"No, just staying straight, keeping my job, cleaning up the mess I've made. It'd probably be easier to list what I'm *not* afraid of."

"Things happen for a reason," she says. "Fate brought us together. You know how many twelve-step programs there are in L.A.?"

"How many?"

"No fuckin' idea. But I bet it's a lot. And we wound up at the same one."

She swirls the tea in her cup, downs it in one gulp as if it were bourbon or something, then sets it down hard on the table in front of her. "Of all the gin joints in all the towns in all the world and... okay, inappropriate reference, but you get the idea."

I laugh. Everything Nikki does makes me laugh. Being on a sitcom for five years may not have made her a decent actor but it sure sharpened her comic timing.

"So... do you have a sponsor?"

"Not yet."

"You do now," she says. "Sobriety isn't easy. I can help you work the program. Maybe even help you avoid making some of the mistakes I made."

"Most of my mistakes involved guys. Put me in a roomful of people and within a minute I'll find the baddest bro there."

"Tell me about it." Nikki turns and gently brushes the hair out of my eyes. "'Ya gotta be careful. This town is full of leeches. I never had anyone looking out for my welfare. Just a bunch of parasites all trying to get rich off me. Including my lovely mother, thank you very much. That bitch actually…'"

A sharp yipping sound interrupts her. It's joined by another and another, followed by short staccato howls that rise and sink in pitch. The effect is primal and frightening, like a cackling coven of witches. We look out into the hills, but see only patches of blackness in between the twinkling lights of the houses.

"Coyotes," she says, sucking hard on the Winston. "Must've made a kill."

"Let's go in. Will you help me run lines?"

• • •

Nikki's sitting on the closed toilet seat holding a script. I'm at my sink, in my mom's long Pearl Jam T-shirt, reciting lines with a mouth full of toothpaste. Wheezer sleeps on top of the wicker hamper, simultaneously purring and wheezing as only Persians can do.

"*Of course I care for you. But this game you're playing is poisoning me,*" I say in between brushing.

"Poisoning *us.*"

"Oh, right. *But this game you're playing is poisoning us.*"

"*You can leave whenever you like,*" Nikki says, playing the part of my love interest.

I rinse out my mouth and spit into the sink.

"*Can I?* Is that right?"

"Yeah, that's the whole scene. You really know this shit."

"I hope so. It helps having someone to run lines with." I wipe my mouth with a towel. "My mom used to rehearse with me. And fyi, she was a *terrible* actress. Sometimes I could barely get through a scene without cracking up. Like, she'd try to do accents. And when the character was mad she'd raise her voice and shake her fist like a villain from an old melodrama."

"My mom used to criticize all my line readings. Like she's an expert or something. Pissed me off."

"Are you close with your mother?" I squeeze moisturizing lotion into my hand and spread it on my face.

"Close? No. Stay away from failed actresses—when they don't get attention, they go apeshit."

"Your mom was an actress?"

"More like a starlet. Never got many lines—she was used mostly for set decoration. She quit the business after a studio head raped her."

"Oh my god. Did she press charges?"

"Naw, in those days, you kept your mouth closed if you knew what was good for you."

"Where is she now?"

"The valley. She lives with some trucker named Frank who beats her up. I hear from them every time my mom tries to off herself, which is usually once a year. But Frank always manages to save her."

I don't know what to say. I think about my own mom again, wondering what she's doing now. I'm sure she's beating herself up, thinking she's failed me. And I guess she has. But it makes me sad to think of her all alone in our ranch house in Kenosha. I'm dying to call her, but the staff at my last rehab place strongly discouraged it, at least for three months.

"Look at you," says Nikki. "No wonder you're famous. Fiery red hair, perfect features, killer figure. With all the shit you put into your body, you're still gorgeous. I used to have looks, but not like you. You got good genes, sister." I smile, embarrassed.

Nikki leans over and smoothes a glob of lotion on my face.

"I don't know about the genes. My dad was alcoholic, so I probably have a predisposition for substance abuse. But that doesn't mean I can't be sober," I say more as a question than a statement.

"Right. Because you're putting your faith in a higher power now."

"Yeah, that higher power stuff. Honestly, I'm not sure I completely get the concept. I try to. I know I'm supposed to embrace it if I want to get well. I wrestle with it because I'm agnostic."

"A higher power can be anything you want it to be," she says. "Anything greater than yourself, outside of your own ego. I call my h.p. 'Zappa'."

I'm not sure what that is, so I smile and nod my head. "Right now I'm putting my faith in a lower power, Wheezer. And we're going to bed." I pick up Wheezer and he puts his paws around my neck. "Goodnight, Nikki."

"Good-night. Sleep tight. Don't let the bedbugs bite."

I think of the ratty sofa bed I slept on last night and wonder if Nikki's little bedtime rhyme is actually a word of warning. I might have to invest in a futon.

Wheezer and I head for my room. *My room.* Two seemingly insignificant words that are surprisingly meaningful to me. I have a safe place to lay my head. And that's something.

• • •

In bed, I listen to the crickets, the only sound I hear. I remember reading somewhere how you can tell how hot it is by their chirping. You just count the number of chirps in fourteen seconds, then add forty to get the temperature. Using my cell phone clock I try this out and come up with seventy-two degrees. That sounds about right.

Then it strikes me how silly it is that I'm actually doing this. Usually nighttime means staring at the ceiling worrying about what the next day will bring, like where I was going to get my drugs from and the lies I needed to keep straight. When I was in rehab I'd hear coughing and wailing and sometimes even physical altercations—plates thrown at walls, horrible obscenities. But tonight it's just crickets. Things are definitely looking up.

# CHAPTER THREE

It's good to be back on the set of *Beverly Hills Banshee*. I'm feeling pretty darned pleased with myself, having arrived *before* my call time, fully rested, and my lines memorized. The brief meet-and-greet between Dan and Nikki this morning went better than expected. Nikki was funny and charming, introducing herself by declaring, "I'm Nikki Barnes and I'm a drug addict. Sober for two years and sixty-two days, but the day is young." Thankfully, Dan has a sense of humor. "Take good care of my girl," he said with a wink. "No one likes a fucked-up banshee."

I'm at the tail end of rehearsing a scene with my romantic interest, Shane Walton, who, despite having the abs, pecs, and face of a Greek god, is actually a smart, down-to-earth guy. The scene we're working is about as subtle as... well, a screaming banshee, but we try to bring as much depth as possible to the script. Judging from my fan mail, the series appeals mostly to teen girls who seem to dig its romantic storylines, supernatural elements, and Shane without his shirt on—not necessarily in that order.

Shane went to Juilliard and has done Shakespeare in the Park. I, on the other hand, didn't go to college and the only thing I've done in the park is crystal meth.

I regret how disrespectful I've been to the pros on this show who take the craft of acting seriously. That's my new goal: to respect the work, be humble, and stop giving the media reasons to hate me. Being famous on TMZ is like being rich in Monopoly.

*Banshee* continues to be one of Netflix's most popular shows, but let's face it, it's not going to win a Peabody. Okay, it *did* win a People's Choice for Favorite New TV Drama in its first season.

"That's better than the Emmy's!" my mom says, always looking on the bright side— "It's from the *people!*" Still, I can learn a lot if I just apply myself and be disciplined. When I'm in the moment and responding intuitively to my acting partner, there's nothing like it. Part of the thrill for me is losing myself in the character, becoming someone else. That's always been effortless for me and has its roots in my home life. Whenever my parents would fight, usually about my dad's drinking, I'd go to my room and act out characters in front of the mirror. It's like another state of consciousness, one I can reach without drugs, and it comforts me.

In high school, I played Masha in Chekhov's *Three Sisters.* The character is quick-tempered, a characteristic I definitely didn't share with her. So Mr. Dawkins, my drama teacher, helped me discover that part of me, however buried it might be. The irony is that once I started using drugs, being quick-tempered became second nature to me. Guess it wasn't as dormant as I thought. I like to think my trouble-making days made me a better actor, but maybe that's just me trying to put a positive spin on a period that caused everyone in my life a great deal of pain.

Now I play Brianna the banshee, an immortal Irish spirit who haunts a Beverly Hills mansion. Shane plays Parker, the wealthy, teenaged son of an industrialist billionaire, who is falling in love with Brianna.

In the scene we're rehearsing, I appear in Parker's bedroom late at night. Wearing a low-cut, diaphanous gown, I'm ethereal as hell. Shane is shirtless, as he is in most scenes.

Parker: I don't care what you are, Brianna. I need to be with you.

Brianna (in my best Irish brogue): Don't you understand? You must leave at once!

Parker: That's not your decision to make.

Brianna: If you loved me, really loved me, you'd...

Parker: Stop, Brianna. You've said enough. No more words.

Shane takes my face in his strong hands and kisses me. Well, at least that's what the script says. In reality, we both tilt our heads in the same direction and meet awkwardly, nose-to-nose.

"We said *I'd* face downstage, not you!" I say.

"I know, I forgot!" says Shane, laughing.

"Dude, you can mess up all afternoon for all I care. I'm just grateful it's not me for a change!"

The crew laughs.

"No worries," says the stage manager. "Time to break anyway. Take fifteen, people."

As I step off the set, I pass Kira Franklin, the lower echelon banshee Danny mentioned as the Actress Most Likely to Steal My Job. She stops me by gently touching my arm.

"I see you haven't lost your magic touch," she says. "You really crushed that scene with Shane."

"Thanks, Kira."

She lowers her voice as she steps closer to me. "I hope you're doing okay. I can't even begin to imagine what you've been through. I'm here if you ever need to talk."

"I may take you up on that," I say, knowing I won't. I'm still uncomfortable around the cast and crew considering the rotten things I've said and done before the hiatus and all. Instead, I join Nikki who's seated in front of the set in a director's chair, watching from the sidelines.

"Keep your eye on that one," she says.

"Who, Kira?" I sit down beside her.

"I don't trust her."

"Really? She was the only one who visited me in rehab. She even brought me a pizza-sized Snooky's Cookie."

Nikki turns to me with her perfected "seriously?" look. I feel like Pollyanna if Pollyanna had track marks on her arms.

I'm about to respond, but am interrupted by a blonde woman who's just entered the set and is heading our way.

"Devon O'Keefe! So good to finally meet you!" she says, giving me an air kiss—mwah!—when she reaches me. She has the freakish look of someone who's had way too much work done. Her fake blonde hair is overly coiffed and she's wearing more makeup than the drag queens in West Hollywood.

I shake her hand, unable to make eye-contact because those collagen-injected lips are pleading for attention.

She looks at me and can clearly tell I have no idea who she is.

"Tammy Robbins," she says, introducing herself. "From *People*. Where shall we chat?"

"Um, actually, I was told no interviews my first week back."

Dan walks over. "That's right, Tammy. We decided no press right now. But in a couple of weeks we'd love to have you back. I'm sure you understand."

"But I was told to be here at 3:30."

"*Really?* Who told you *that?*" he asks.

"I don't know—someone from the show set it up with my assistant."

"There's obviously been some sort of mix-up." Dan looks around for someone who might know something but can't spot anyone.

"That's too bad," she says. "We're also doing a piece on TV's top twenty producers and I was hoping to get a quote from Devon on how you're the best thing since cauliflower pizza."

Dan laughs. "Ah, the power of flattery." He turns to me. "Devon, how do you feel about a quick interview so Tammy won't have to leave here empty-handed?"

I hate interviews. I'm often misquoted and even when I'm not, they're usually slanted so I come off as either bitchy, self-centered, or a total airhead. I really don't want to give Apocalips the interview, but I also don't want to make waves with Dan on my second day back. I look at Nikki and she frowns, then nods her head, confirming I'm screwed and have no choice.

"Sure," I say.

"Super!" says Dan. "Then I'll leave you two alone." He has his assistant bring over bottled water for each of us and he's off. Tammy takes a seat next to me so I'm between her and Nikki.

"I saw some of your rehearsal," she says. "Looks like the *Parkanna* romance is really heating up."

I wince at the nickname our two characters have been given by the fans. "Yes, we could only sustain the flirting for so long."

"Does the chemistry ever cross over into your off-screen lives?"

Okay, now I'm pissed. Everyone knows Shane is married. While he's played a nineteen-year-old on the show for four seasons, he's now actually twenty-six. I decide to take the high road.

"Well, as you know, Shane is married, so no, that's not even a possibility. And I'm friends with his gorgeous wife so..."

"Is it difficult to do love scenes without drugs or alcohol to loosen things up?"

"Why, what've you got?" I ask.

Nikki lets out a laugh but the humorless Tammy Robbins just carries on.

"I mean, are you worried about staying sober, given the enormous pressure that's on you at this point in your career?"

"I'm sorry," Nikki says, leaning over. "We didn't realize the interview was headed in this direction."

Tammy doesn't even turn to address Nikki, just speaks directly to me.

"Honey, I'm sure you know they're saying some terribly unflattering things about you in the fan blogs. This is your opportunity to reach out to your following, let them know what you're all about. Garner some sympathy."

"I understand that, but..."

"Unless you *want* to be lumped in with the Lindsays and Britneys and both Demies."

"Interview's over," Nikki says, standing up and holding out her hand. "Goodbye."

Trout Pout doesn't shake it, just says, "I'm sorry?"

"Devon's not demeaning herself by answering your tacky questions. When she's ready to talk seriously about her sobriety you'll hear her on Howard Stern."

"And you are?" Tammy asks.

"I'm her manager. Nikki Barnes." *Manager?*

The name registers with Tammy.

"Nikki Barnes! Of course! Nice to see you, Nikki."

I have no idea what's going on in Tammy's scheming little mind because her forehead is botoxed within an inch of her life. But my guess is her wheels are spinning like crazy. Her tone changes dramatically.

"I apologize to both of you if any of my questions were impertinent."

"Noted," says Nikki.

"I do have a proposition I'd like to run by you, though." Yep, here it comes.

"Forget today's interview," she says. "I'd like to do a more comprehensive feature story on the two of you."

"No friggin' way," says Nikki.

"Hear me out. I find it fascinating that you, of all people, are managing Devon's career. Two actresses at different stages of their careers, both battling addictions."

"That's nobody's business," I say in protest.

"Maybe it should be. Think of all the young people who could benefit from what you have to say. Do you know that over four thousand people under age twenty-one die each year from alcohol-related car crashes, homicides, suicides, alcohol poisoning, and other injuries?"

Whoa. Someone's done her homework.

I sincerely consider this. I like the idea that teens could actually benefit from the poor choices I've made. I look at Nikki blankly.

"We'll think about it," she says.

"Nikki, trust me. This story can make both of you look like the brave survivors you are. You can't buy publicity like that. I may even be able to get you the cover."

"Let's talk tomorrow," Nikki says. "We need the night to think about it. I want to make sure Devon's totally comfortable with whatever she decides."

"You got it," Tammy says and after we all air-kiss again, she's outta there.

I'm impressed by the way Nikki's handled things. If my mom had been in charge she would've caved instantly; she wasn't the savviest businesswoman. But Nikki was firm and professional, and I'm struck by how safe she makes me feel. Even screaming banshees need nurturing sometimes.

• • •

Driving home through the canyon, an eerie fog surrounds us as we climb the winding streets of the hills. I'm used to fog—at least the kind that comes out of machines to create an air of mystery. But real fog is much scarier—I don't like the thought of a hidden anything.

"God, I can barely see two feet in front of my face," I say.

"You're doing fine."

"I am, aren't I?" And not just my driving. Day two at work and not only was I totally prepared, I was sober. I'd say any day that I don't barf all over my co-workers is a step in the right direction. "It feels good to do an honest day's work."

"I wouldn't know. It's been ages since I've acted."

"How come?"

"I've burned way too many bridges. No one wants to work with someone with a history like mine."

"I do. You're my manager now, huh?"

"I pulled that outta my ass because I couldn't stand to see frozen face try to manipulate you like that. But if you're not comfortable with—"

"No, I *am*. I *love* the idea of you as my manager. And my sponsor." At least I think I do. It's all happened so fast.

"Really?" Nikki seems pleased.

I nod.

Suddenly, a coyote juts out right in front of my car. He's scraggly and gray with a black nose and wide, pointed ears.

"Whoa!"

I slam on my brakes. The coyote and I make eye contact, then he darts off into the night. Nikki and I continue climbing the hill, my heart pounding.

• • •

Southern Californians call this kind of morning "June Gloom," where the sky is overcast and the temperature is cool. But *emotionally,* nothing could be further from the truth. One of the new little joys in my life is the act of waking up sober. No pounding headache, no horrible taste in my mouth from drugs or alcohol. No sore jaw from clenching my teeth all night. I wake feeling clear-headed, and actually look forward to what the day has to offer.

At least at first. If I allow myself to linger too long in bed, my mind becomes an active volcano of negative thoughts. I either ruminate (a word one of my shrinks was fond of) about the past—all the things I wish I'd done differently—or fantasize about the future— money troubles, re-lapsing, diseases I'm sure I have. The key is to get up before my mind has a chance to ambush my good mood. I look around for Wheezer but he's off somewhere, exploring all the nooks and crannies of his new home.

Getting dressed, I decide to nix my usual jeans and T-shirt look, which seem like remnants of the old Devon, the one whose appearance always took a back seat to more important things—like drugs. I select a white silk blouse and cream-colored, high-waisted linen slacks. More Courtney Cox than Courtney Love. I figure if I'm going to act more professional, I might as well dress the part.

• • •

Downstairs, I pull a cup of yogurt out of the fridge. I can hear Nikki in the living room negotiating with Tammy Robbins on the phone.

"We get final approval on the article or we don't do it at all. Photo approval too," she says. "Why? Because I don't want some asshole photographer trying to make us look like Keith Richards, that's why." Nikki. Gotta love her way with words.

I grab a spoon and sit down at the kitchen table, which, as usual, is filthy. I push away a plate that has the remains of congealed egg yolk on it. At the center is a stubbed-out cigarette butt. I can hear Nikki pacing as the conversation gets more heated.

"Bullshit, Tammy. Don't tell me you never relinquish creative control because I know better. It's done all the time, only no one ever admits it."

I notice a swarm of ants devouring a stale, half-eaten Pop Tart Nikki left on a plate. I know I should probably find some Raid and clean it up but I'm so grossed out and it's way too early to be dealing with this. I just pick up my yogurt, slide open the door to the patio and step outside. Before I close the door, I can hear Nikki yelling a triumphant, "Yessss!!!"

I sit on a lounge chair facing a pool that's filled with dark green muck. A condom floats on the surface, making me want to gag. I get up and reverse the chair to face the lovely hills, the fog still creeping over them. I can hear Andy Chiu's Chinese music wafting from next door, calming me, as I'm sure it calms him. And that's when I see something I'll never be able to un-see for the rest of my life. I let out a shriek. A few feet in front of me, lying crumpled on the stone patio in a puddle of blood is the mutilated body of Wheezer. I turn away and double over, trying not to vomit.

"Oh my god!" I fall to my knees, sobbing like a widow in a war-torn country. I hear the door slide open and Nikki comes running out.

"What's going on?"

I can no longer form words, just point in the general direction of Wheezer.

Nikki lets out her own shriek, then turns her back on the bloody mess that's Wheezer, her hands covering her mouth. "Oh, Jesus," she says, then, "Coyotes. I should have warned you not to let Wheezer out."

"I didn't. He's not an outdoor cat. He must've climbed out my bedroom window. I left it open a crack—I didn't think he'd be able to squeeze through." I try to stand but my shaky knees make me unsteady so I sit on the lounge chair. I can't stop crying. Unwanted images assault my mind, illustrating what Wheezer must've suffered. Nikki comes over and puts her arms around me.

I grab onto her and become an hysterical crying machine, slobbering snot and tears all over her T-shirt with its familiar smell of cigarette smoke.

"Is everything okay?"

I look up and see a man with a gray ponytail wearing only pajama-style pants climbing over the fence. "I heard screams," he adds.

"Andy," Nikki says. "The coyotes got my friend's cat."

"I am so sorry, young lady," he says and bows his head reverently. I nod.

Andy finds a large black trash bag on the patio and places it over the carnage.

"Man, oh, man. Why don't you take her inside," he says to Nikki. "I'll take care of this for you."

"Thanks, Andy," Nikki says. "I don't think either of us can deal with it right now."

I manage to stop crying for a moment as Nikki helps me to my feet and leads me inside. My body's numb; I have to actually concentrate to get my feet to step one in front of the other. But my mind isn't numb; it's reeling, wondering how I'll ever get rid of an image so grisly it wipes out all others.

• • •

I'm curled up in a ball on the living room couch. Nikki brings me a glass of water and I'm only half-kidding when I say, "Thanks, but what I really need is vodka." I sit up and accept the water with shaky hands.

"Don't even joke about that," she says and sits down next to me.

"I can't believe he's dead. My little Wheezer, my security blanket. What am I gonna do without him?"

"For starters, sob your eyes out. The shortest way to the other side of grief is *through*." I'm pretty sure this is another AA saying. I wonder if two people could carry on an entire conversation using only twelve-step aphorisms. I also wonder how my mind is able to come up with these kind of insights during moments of great anguish like this.

I turn to Nikki. "What's the *second* shortest way to the other side of grief?"

"I think we both know the answer to that, but for you that's not an option. Hold on a sec."

Nikki gets up and pulls a paperback from a bookshelf in the entertainment center. I'd perused these books yesterday and they resembled the Self Help section of Barnes and Noble—drug abuse, alcoholism, bulimia, anorexia, co-dependency, hypnosis, primal screams, feminism, nutrition, exercise, depression, anxiety, Christianity, parenting, being your own best friend because no one else can stand to be near your sorry ass—the whole nine yards. A bibliography of Nikki's tormented life.

"Here. Listen to this," Nikki says, reading from a dog-eared paperback as she walks back to the couch. She hits me with a barrage of words that I'm unable to fully take in. But the gist of it is this—don't suppress sadness. Because you're just delaying the inevitable. The more you suppress grief, the more likely it will slip out in unconscious ways at unwanted times. Or worse, the feelings will be turned inward, causing depression.

"I get it. And you don't have to worry. I'll cry, not get high."

"Excellent." Nikki goes over to her landline phone on the side table. It's red and shaped like a pair of lips. "Let me call the show. You can't go in today."

"I have to. I've got a rehearsal this morning and we're shooting a promo this afternoon. Dan'll totally freak."

"Not if I explain what happened. How can they expect you to work after something like this?"

"You don't understand. I've lied to them so many times before. If I don't show up, they'll think I'm using again." I take a sip of water and stand up. I notice my slacks are dirty from kneeling on the patio concrete. "I've gotta change real quick. I can't be late," I say and head upstairs.

"Okay, but promise you'll call if you get in trouble. I can Uber it and be there in half an hour."

"Thanks," I yell down to her. "Really, though. I'm good. I'm good."

• • •

I'm not good. I'm crying like a maniac as I drive through Hollywood. I really shouldn't be behind the wheel of a car. I keep stealing looks at photos of Wheezer on my phone and each one makes me that much more upset. Not paying attention to the road, I veer to the right and onto the sidewalk, almost hitting a homeless encampment on La Brea. "Sorry!" I yell as I get back on the road. That's just what I need—vehicular manslaughter added to my bio.

As I reach the front gate of the studio I grab my sunglasses and am reminded how many times I've used them in the past to hide my druggy eyes after a long night of partying. Thankfully, I'm able to make it to my dressing room without running into anyone from the show. I'm hit with a slightly rancid smell and realize it's from the vase of flowers the crew gave me a couple of days ago on my first day back. I pour out the old water, replace it with water from the tap and set it down on my coffee table. The bouquet suddenly looks more like a funeral arrangement than a welcome back gift. Wheezer loved flowers. I remember how he once spilled water all over my laptop when he knocked over a vase of flowers by rubbing his face all over the pollen. I lost all my files and had to shell out over a thousand bucks on a new computer, but never once did I blame him. He was being a cat. That's what cats do. I start crying again.

No. I can't do this. I've got twenty minutes to pull myself together before rehearsal begins. I begin to prioritize. The first thing I need to do is calm the hell down, or I'll blow my lines at rehearsal. And I can't look upset in front of everyone because they'll assume the worst. How do I calm down? Normally—if there is such a thing as normal in my life—I'd call my mom. I realize I'm supposed to keep her out of the picture for a few months but with what's happened this morning I don't think anyone would blame me. I need to hear a familiar voice. I need someone to tell me everything's going to be all right when I know it isn't.

I sit down in front of my vanity mirror and dial her number. As soon as I hear her voice I start crying.

"Hi, Mom..."

"Oh honey, you sound awful, what's wrong?"

"Wheezer's dead." I manage to choke out my words in between sobs. "A coyote..."

"What? Oh my god! Are you okay?"

"No. I'm not. I'm at work and I'm hysterical." I look at my distressed face in the mirror and can find no trace of a pretty banshee. My anxiety ratchets up a notch or two. "I don't know what to do."

"See, honey, this is why I need to be with you," she says in a voice that sounds more irritated than calming. "Those goddamn social workers think they know best, but what you need right now is your mother and a big hug."

"I know, Mom, I know. But you're not here and I need to get a hold of myself. So how do I do that?"

"Valium."

"Yeah, right."

"No, I'm serious. You need to pop a Valium. Do you have any?"

"What? No! I'm in *recovery!*"

"I'm not telling you to shoot up, for cryin' out loud, I'm just saying take a Valium. It's a prescription drug—everybody takes them."

"Oh god, Mom, you don't get it, do you? I'm an *addict*. I can't take *any* substance; why would you even suggest that?" I stand up and feel like pacing but my dressing room's way too small for that. Instead, I rock back and forth, shifting from foot to foot.

"Your cat was just killed! Look, you called me and asked—"

"Never mind, Mom. This wasn't a good idea. I have to go. Bye."

I end the call and swear never to phone her again until I'm like, fifty. I don't know what to do with my body. I sit down, stand up, crouch on the floor. My dressing room feels like a tiny dollhouse that I'm trapped inside of. Back to prioritizing. Calming down is no longer an option—I'm more keyed-up than before the call. Now I just need to create the *illusion* I'm okay.

I look in the mirror again and it's not a pretty sight. My face is a blotchy mess and my eyes are swollen and red. Thankfully, I always carry a tube of Preparation H in my purse for just this purpose. Don't laugh. It restricts the blood vessels, which gets rid of the redness, and it contains hydrocortisone, which reduces puffiness. My actor friends swear by it, though some claim it's a placebo—that its effectiveness is just an urban legend. In any case, I need all the help I can get so I frantically grab my bag and dig inside, tossing out my brush, my lipstick, my gum.

I find it all right, but I also find something else: a joint. There it is, as real as can be. I have no idea how it got there. I thought I got rid of all my drugs when I went to rehab but I suppose this little number could have managed to survive the purge. To be honest, I don't remember what I had or what I threw out—my memory is pretty hazy considering all the drama and drugs going on at the time. Or maybe someone put it in there. Maybe someone's testing me, or worse, trying to sabotage my sobriety. I'm not sure. Maybe I'm being paranoid. I take the joint and go over to the toilet to flush it down.

But first, I hold it up to my nose and smell it. The earthy scent is nice and familiar. The joint is like the drug version of comfort food, a stoner's version of tomato soup and a grilled cheese sandwich. I think of a higher power and wait for it to give me the strength to flush it down the toilet. But apparently the higher power is on a break, or maybe tending to some other, more important junkie.

I think of calling Nikki, my sponsor. But I don't. I light it. I take one hit, then another. I hold the warm smoke in my lungs for as long as I can before exhaling. It's harsh, much harsher than usual and it has a bitter aftertaste. I know in a few minutes I'll feel better, less stressed. Then I remember the urine test and I'm instantly panicky. All I feel is fear. And shame. For being weak. For being me.

• • •

It takes a few minutes to realize the weed didn't calm me down at all. Don't know why. I can feel my pulse speed up and picture my blood cascading through my veins like the Colorado rapids. Instead of the mellow buzz I was expecting, I'm feeling a manic high. Full of energy. Lots of energy. Gotta move. Gotta keep moving.

• • •

In the make-up chair, I feel great but can hardly sit still. I look in the mirror and my pupils are seriously dilated. Pat is painfully slow with the eyebrow pencil. At one point I grab it from her and use it myself. She looks pissed off.

"You all right, Dev?" she asks.

"I'm fine. Just want to get on stage and do this promo. Please hurry up."

"We've got plenty of time. You're not due on set until..."

"Please don't argue with me." Shit. How rude. I can't help myself. I apologize. Pat says, "No worries," then there's this uncomfortable silence as she continues to make me up. My legs are twitching. The back of my head is tingling. What is going on? Pot never affected me this way before. Is it because I've been sober for a month? Can't wait to get up and start moving, acting. I am Brianna! Sexy and supernatural! Banshee power, bitches, ha ha!

• • •

As I walk to the set, almost running, Shane greets me.

"Hey, Dev. What's up? You look... *different*." What does that even mean? He must sense I'm high. Play it cool.

"Ready to work. That's all. Work, work, work."

"I guess," he sort of half smiles. "You sure you're okay? You seem kinda tense."

I stop walking, grab him by the arm. "My cat got torn apart by wild coyotes! I'm a little upset, okay?" Jeez, total overreaction. Now for sure he knows I'm high. Just keep moving, get to the set.

"Gosh, I'm sorry, Dev," I hear him say behind me. On set now. Standing on a platform with a green screen behind me. They're shooting me from the waist up. Huge fans blow my hair. Looks like I'm flying.

The director asks me if I want to rehearse. "No, it's only a couple of lines—let's just shoot it."

Dan is watching me from the sidelines like a hawk. And hawks are birds of prey; it's only a matter of time before he attacks. I try to act as normal as possible but I'm having a hard time concentrating. My thoughts are jumbled, but I remember the script words just fine and feel oddly powerful, even euphoric. I try my best to focus. Just get the words out, Devon, you know them. I look directly at the camera, stare that mother down.

I spit out the lines in my Irish brogue like I mean them. It's a miracle I get them right, since my head is in a fog.

"'Tis not the howlin' wind on a stormy night, nor the whistle of a faraway train. The sound you hear 'tis me – the cry of the fallen goddess, the wail of the banshee!" Dan smiles, pleased I know my lines. I open my mouth and emit a long, eerie, high-pitched keening. The cry is cathartic and seems to come from a place so deep and dark, I never knew it existed. I'm in love with the way it resonates in my throat then blasts out of my mouth, shattering the air. I indulge in the moment, letting the shrill sound gather in intensity. When I'm done I look up and the crew is just standing there, looking stunned. Dan's mouth is actually hanging open—did that sound come from her? I'm pretty sure I impressed everyone but there's the chance I just weirded them out. I can't tell.

"One more for safety?" I ask.

"No, we're good, we're good," says the director. I walk back to my dressing room in silence, everyone staring at me as I go. Or am I just being paranoid?

# CHAPTER FOUR

Nikki and I are having dinner at the bottom of the canyon in the bohemian restaurant, Pace. I pronounced it as rhyming with "race" until Nikki informed me it's pah-chay. It means "peace" in Italian according to the owner who's a friend of Nikki's. He seats us in a dark corner and I'm feeling a bit claustrophobic. Nikki's chowing down on a pesto and arugula pizza; I ordered a salad, but all I can do is pick at it. I have no appetite.

"How are you feeling now?" Nikki asks.

"Depressed. Tired."

"You're beating yourself up," Nikki says, pulling a string of cheese from her pizza and into her mouth.

"Of course I am. Why couldn't I have just flushed that joint down the toilet?"

"Because your cat just died and it was there. Too easy not to."

"I thought I was stronger than that."

"Look, for every two steps forward, you take one step back. It's just the natural flow of recovery."

"I thought I got rid of all my drugs. Someone must've put that joint there."

"Huh."

"No, really. What if it was a test? Anyone from the show could've planted it there. Dan. Kira. Even Shane. Someone whose life would improve if I were out of the picture."

"I guess it's possible. But no one forced you to smoke it. You have to take responsibility for that."

"I do. But I think it was laced with something because I feel so bugged out. And I know I wouldn't have had coco puffs on my own."

"Coco puffs? What the fuck?"

"Yeah, that's what it's called when you lace a joint with cocaine or crack."

"Kids say the darndest things," Nikki deadpans.

The waiter stops by our table. "How're you ladies doing?"

"Fabulous," Nikki says, looking up at him and smiling flirtatiously even though he's half her age.

He looks ill-at-ease as he pulls a folded piece of paper out of his apron pocket. "Um, I hope this is cool, but can I..."

"You want an autograph?" Nikki asks as she takes the paper from him. "Her, me or both?"

"Actually, no." He points at the paper, a flyer. "I'm in a new play at the Farrell Theatre on Santa Monica Boulevard? It's called *Neurotica* and it's a Jungian hejira from the conscious world into the landscape of the libido."

"Uh-huh," Nikki says. She and I avoid each other's eyes.

"I recognized you two and thought maybe you could come see it, or pass the word on to some of your friends in the industry."

"Uh-huh," Nikki says again. "Is this the same play as the one the valet guy mentioned on the way in?" She pulls out another flyer from her bag.

"Seth? No, his is a musical. Kinda kitschy, I hear. This one's pretty profound."

"Uh-huh," Nikki says for the third time. She looks at the flyer, then back at the waiter. "Good luck with it. And could we have the check, please?"

"No problem," he says, looking a little embarrassed. "Coming right up." He leaves the flyer on the table and heads off.

Nikki waits until he's out-of-sight, then cracks up. "This town," she says.

I smile, but am unable to laugh. What's the expression—*there but for the grace of God go I?* The thought of waiting on tables to pay the bills and trying to cajole people into seeing me in a local play is just too grim at the moment.

"What am I going to do about my drug test, Nikki?"

"Please. You can buy drug-free concentrated urine online."

"You can?"

"Uh-huh. Used to be a staple on my shopping list: whiskey, Häagen Dazs, clean piss." She finishes off the last bite of her pizza, talks with her mouth full. "But you're not doing that."

"I'm not?"

"No, you're marching straight into Dan's office tomorrow morning and telling him the truth."

"Are you *insane?*"

"Once you start lying, you're screwed. You'll be an addict again before you can say Tatum O'Neal."

"Who's that?"

"Exactly."

"But Dan'll fire me."

"He will for sure if the test comes back positive. But if you go to him first you have a chance he'll respect your honesty. And if you *do* get fired, life goes on. Actions have consequences. Remember, sweetie, your fate is in the hands of a higher power now."

I pick at my salad with my fork. "Yeah let's hope that higher power can land me another series."

•  •  •

"Two days?" Dan says, raising his voice. "What the fuck is *that?* Jesus, you're not even trying!"

We're on the back lot; I suggested we take a walk so we could talk. I thought maybe being out in public might prevent him from blowing up. Guess I was wrong.

"Please don't yell at me."

He lowers his voice. "I went to bat for you and this is how you repay me?"

"I know. I'm sorry."

"Gee, that's some consolation. I'm sure the folks at Netflix will be thrilled."

"Why do they have to know?"

"Didn't you read your contract? The results of your drug tests are sent to them. They have the right to terminate you based on those results."

"Nobody told me. My mom reads my contracts."

"I knew your moving in with that junkie was a bad idea." I stop walking and step in front of Dan, blocking his path.

"Nikki had nothing to do with this. In fact she's the one who encouraged me to tell you the truth. She even persuaded me to go to an extra NA meeting last night after dinner."

"Well, that's something, I guess." He steps around me, continues walking.

A golf cart with two women dressed like aliens passes us by in case I need reminding of how strange my life is.

"Please give me one more chance, Dan. I swear it won't happen again. It was just 'cause of Wheezer. That cat was the only one who stood by me when things got bad."

"Yes, pets tend to love indiscriminately. I suggest you surround yourself with lots of them. It's people you might want to avoid."

Now he's getting mean. I don't know how to respond so we keep walking. Finally he speaks.

"One more chance. But I can't guarantee the bosses will agree."

I hug Dan. He tenses up, doesn't hug me back.

"Thank you. I promise you won't regret it." I'm so grateful, tears well up in my eyes.

"Jesus, don't start crying," he says. "We've got a scene to shoot."

• • •

"You sure you're okay?" Pat says to me as she applies my make-up. "Your hands are shaking worse than mine the time I had to put pancake on Chris Hemsworth's tuchus."

"I'm fine."

"Hey, this stuff usually kills. Don't I even get a smile?"

"I'm sorry, Pat," I say as quietly as possible. There are actors on either side of me, getting made-up. "I feel really shitty and I have no idea why."

"Really? No idea?" We look at each other in the mirror. Pat's a recovering alcoholic, twenty years sober.

"Your secret's safe with me," she says in a near-whisper. She gets me a bottle of water. "Here, drink this. I think you're dehydrated—your skin's dry as hell."

I drink a few slugs of water, then take a couple of deep breaths but can't stop shaking.

"What are you feeling exactly?" asks Pat.

"Depressed. Anxious. Achy. I've got the chills."

"Tell Dan you've got the flu. They can probably juggle the schedule."

"No, no, I can't do that."

The stage manager pops his head in the room. "Five minutes, Devon!"

I remove my bib, get up from the chair and head for my dressing room.

• • •

I text Nikki but there's no response, so I call her landline and get her archaic answering machine. Why she still has a landline is beyond me—maybe it's just that it would take too much energy to cancel the service. Or maybe she gets comfort from surrounding herself with things from the past, when she was in her prime. That would explain the "décor"—and I use the term loosely—of her house.

"Nikki, it's me. If you're there, pick up." I wait a moment. Nothing. "Okay, look, I need your help. I couldn't sleep at all last night and today

I'm feeling sick. I don't know what's wrong with me, and you have to believe me—I didn't take anything. I'm supposed to be on the set in like two minutes and—hold on a sec." I take a swig of water, then another. "Sorry—my mouth feels like the Mojave. Anyway, I'm *this* close to trying to scrounge up something that'll make me feel normal again. There's a gaffer on the crew who sometimes carries. I could try him. Never mind, bad idea. Let's see..." I check the time on my phone. "It's almost ten o'clock. If you get this message please come to soundstage three."

• • •

On the way to the set I pass Coop the gaffer. He's winding a cable from hand to elbow. He looks pleasantly stoned as usual—sleepy eyes, Mona Lisa smile, his long hair partially covering his face.

"What's up, buttercup?" he says to me. "Everything copacetic?" He can tell I'm not myself.

"I think I may be coming down with something. But I'm okay."

"Let me know if you need anything. I'm a freakin' drug store."

I was afraid of that. I stand there for what feels like forever, deciding what to do.

"I'm in recovery," I finally say.

"Yeah, recovery. Same as the last time you hit me up."

"This time it's for real. And I'm not hitting you up for anything."

"Cool. So I guess we're done here then, huh?"

"I guess so." I start to walk away, then stop. "Coop—in the future it'd be a good idea if we stayed away from each other. I don't need any temptations."

"Wouldn't be the first time an attractive young lady said that to me," he says, grinning.

• • •

Despite all the lights on the set I have the chills. I take my place at the edge of the set in my director's chair, across from Shane and Kira who are having a conversation. They sneak looks at me like I have leprosy or something. We wait for the director to show up. The fact that he's not here already concerns me. Something's going on.

A therapist in rehab taught me a technique for when I feel anxious. I get up and find a dark empty space behind the set. I close my eyes and exhale deeply, then take a long, slow breath in through my nose, filling my lower lungs, then my upper ones. I hold my breath for a count of three, then exhale slowly through my pursed lips while relaxing the muscles in my jaw, shoulders and stomach. I repeat the process and it seems to work; in a few minutes I feel calmer.

Now I just need a distraction. I try some creative visualization, conjuring up images of pleasant times from my past. My dad reading *The Wind and the Willows* to me when I was a kid; my mom taking me to see the Christmas windows at Marshall Fields. But I can't seem to stay with these memories for long. I open my eyes and wonder how I got here? How did a nice midwestern girl from Kenosha grow up to become an addict, an alcoholic, liar, and thief?

I think back to about six years ago when I was seventeen. My dad had recently died and our home was suddenly quiet. No bickering between my parents, no drunken outbursts from my dad. My depressed mom spent her nights at the kitchen table, surrounded by unpaid bills and debt.

School was a haven for me, an invigorating place where my only fear was getting an A-. While I wasn't in the popular crowd, I found my place with the theatre kids who, like me, were quirky non-conformists—and budding neurotics. I dreamt of someday acting in a professional play in Milwaukee or better yet, Chicago. At that time, talent scouts from Hollywood were searching the country for just the right girl to play the lead in a TeenNick sitcom called *Killin' It,* about a high school girl who leads a double life as a stand-up comic.

I realize now that searches like this are done mostly for publicity; they could've just as easily cast the role from the thousands of desperate girls who flock to L.A. every year seeking fame, many trying to escape the boredom of their small towns or abuse in their homes. The ones you see on Hollywood Boulevard, looking listless and hungry. But the producers came to see me in my high school's production of, yes, *Our Town*, and the next thing you know, they're flying me and my mom out here for a screen test.

I lost the part to Mia Reese, but was cast in a comedic supporting role as her best friend, Isabella, a goodie-goodie teacher's pet. My dad had just passed away so moving to L.A. with mom made sense, the only thing keeping us in Wisconsin being school. I got a diploma anyway, by taking the GED.

While *Killin' It* was panned by the critics, it became a hit with audiences. And Isabella caught on with fans, so the writers expanded the part for the second season. This wasn't a problem until the tabloids decided to stir things up by writing that Mia and I had vicious "cat fights" on set, which was totally untrue. They wrote that Mia resented me because her stand-up comic wasn't getting as many laughs as her sidekick.

When the opportunity popped up for me to play the lead role of Brianna in the new Netflix series, *Beverly Hills Banshee*, it seemed like the right move at the right time. My agent was able to get me out of my *Killin' It* contract and I began my new work almost immediately.

Fame is something I never even thought about back home. The suddenness of it created a lot of pressure, and as everyone now knows, I didn't handle it well. The L.A. crowd seemed so hip—their clothes, their lingo, the cars they drove. When my agent suggested I lose ten pounds despite the fact that I wasn't remotely overweight, I felt like I was from another planet. Suddenly, I missed my theatre friends back home—the kids who accepted me for who I was.

My first mistake was to fall in love with a well-known actor who had a guest-starring role on the first season of *Banshee*. We slept together on our second date—my first time—and I was convinced I was in love. Within weeks, *his* drug problem became *our* drug problem.

My mom was too consumed in an affair of her own to notice I badly needed some parenting. She fell hard for some hotshot music exec who apparently thought it was perfectly appropriate for forty-somethings to go club-hopping every night. This was the first guy she dated since my dad died and she threw herself into the relationship. I think she was flattered that some Hollywood mogul would find a midwestern mom attractive. His name was Charles but I liked calling him Chuck, or Chucky, because he hated it.

Around this time, I began shoplifting as a—subconscious, I suppose—way to get mom's attention. I was caught stealing a four hundred and twenty dollar Alexander McQueen silk scarf. I don't wear scarves. And it wasn't my color, although it would've made a nice accent to the orange jumpsuit I later wore as I picked up trash along the highway.

When my drug use became a problem at work I was forced to go into rehab—one of those pricey places in Malibu. There's nothing quite like an ocean view to help make detox bearable. I received excellent counseling there and my soul felt nourished. When I left, I was confident and eager to work.

But I wasn't prepared to be instantly dumped by my famous boyfriend who lost interest after I told him I needed to stop partying. I rebounded with another actor, my second mistake. This one really stole my heart—he was funny and gentle and, as I would soon find out, gay. No need to Google that one, he came out of the closet quite publicly—on a morning talk show. I found out about it on Twitter.

I have no words to describe how it feels to be publicly humiliated. To hear a comedian speak your name on TV followed by bursts of derisive laughter. Again, I didn't handle things well. More drugs, more escapades. And around this time, my mom got dumped. In the classic Hollywood tradition, her lover traded her in for a younger model. And I mean that literally—a *super*model who was half his age and weighed like ninety pounds.

Riddled with guilt and now with lots of time on her hands, my mother suddenly decided to become Mom of the Year. But I was furious at her for not being there when I needed her, and her constant presence only seemed to make things worse between us. We fought constantly, and I was seriously out-of-control. Another round of rehab, this one in Palm

Springs—nothing quite like a desert view to make detox bearable—and well, now I'm up-to-date.

I realize I've just done exactly what I said I wouldn't do—rehash my sordid past. I suppose a part of me feels compelled to justify my bad behavior—not make excuses exactly, but try and explain how easy it is, given the right circumstances, for someone's life to spiral out-of-control. Like mine, for instance.

I'm standing here trying to stop shaking, craving a line of coke like a needy comic craves a laugh. I return to my chair. The vibe is tense, the crew standing around, waiting. Something is up, something's definitely up. As my mom often says, quoting one of her favorite Kurt Cobain songs, "Just because you're paranoid don't mean they're not after you."

Finally, Dan enters the soundstage with the director. He looks serious. Shane whispers something to Kira and she whispers back. Dan comes over to me, and in a low voice says, "I need to talk to you."

"Okay."

"Not here. In my office."

"Here is fine. I don't care if the whisper twins hear." I shoot a nasty look at Shane and Kira.

"Devon, let's not make this harder than it has to be. Please, let's just go to my office."

Now I'm feeling *really* paranoid and my ego is on the line. So I decide to make a stand.

"They can hear anything you have to say to me. We're all part of this one big happy family, aren't we?" Sarcasm is rarely a good idea in these situations but I'm on a roll, making one bad choice after another. Can't seem to help myself. I stand up, get in Dan's face.

"So what's the scoop, Mr. Producer?"

He looks around the set, clearly uncomfortable. All the crew is standing around with nothing to do but listen and of course, pretend *not* to listen.

Dan inhales deeply then is out with it. "Your drug test came back. You tested positive for marijuana and..."

"As I expected," I say. "Big deal. I smoked pot like everyone else on the planet. So what happens now?"

"Please, let me finish. We did additional tests and found crack cocaine in your system.

"What? I smoked *one joint*—I told you that, that's all!"

"Then it was one joint laced with cocaine."

"That's crazy!" I say, but actually it makes perfect sense. The pot affected me just like cocaine and now I feel like I'm in withdrawal. Someone spiked that joint and put it in my purse.

"Danny, you've got to believe me. Someone's setting me up."

"It's never your fault, is it, Devon?"

"This time it isn't, I swear!"

Kira whispers something to Shane and he nods. I storm over to her.

"What did you say, bitch?"

"Nothing, it was..."

"You got something to say to me, say it to my face!"

Shane stands up, gets between Kira and me.

"Chill, Devon. We all just want what's best for the show, that's all."

"Oh, I get it. Get me out of the picture and then everything will be all right." I push Shane aside and get in Kira's face.

"You just couldn't wait to take over, could you, Kira? I hope you're happy! Your little plan worked!"

"Devon, calm down," Dan says. Then I see him walk toward the security guards.

"I don't know what you're talking about," Kira says. "If you're accusing me of something, you're really messed up. You need help."

"Oh, *I* need help? I don't think so! I'm the one who just spent thirty days in rehab—I'm fine—it's people like *you* who need help—people who are trying to derail me." I give Kira a little push. I know, not smart. Plus she's in one of those flimsy directors chairs and, well, it goes over. And now all hell breaks lose. Shane helps Kira off the floor and checks to see if she's okay. Looks like her lip is bleeding. Dan's on the phone. Two beefy security guards come toward me. I try to dodge them, but they manage to out-maneuver me and despite my yelling and kicking, they get me in some sort of wrestling hold, with my arm behind my back and lead me out.

"It's not my fault!" I yell. "Leave me alone! Get off me!" And it all sounds so melodramatic that embarrassment almost overtakes my anger. Almost. Then I hear a clarion voice behind me.

"Devon, stop it!"

I look up and it's Nikki. I don't know how long she's been standing there or what she's seen, but I immediately go limp, stop fighting. The guards relax their grip, but still hold me.

"Nikki," I whisper. She drops her purse and walks over to me. The guards release me and I slump to the floor. Nikki gets down on her knees and puts her arms around me. She holds me for quite a while in silence while everyone stands around, gaping.

When she lets go of me, she turns to the others and says, "She'll be fine. Please. Let me take her home."

Dan nods at the security guards. They step back.

"Don't worry, sweetie. Let's go home. This'll all get sorted out." She gets her purse, then helps me up. We start to walk out, past the gawking crew.

"She's not well, guys. Jeez, give her a little respect," Nikki says. The crew sheepishly shuffles away. Shane comes up and plants a kiss on my forehead.

"You get better. We need you here." I nod and smile. I look over to where Kira was and see she's gone. As we pass the craft services table, Nikki grabs a donut, bites into it. "Mmm, Krispy Kremes." She snags another and we're out of there.

# CHAPTER FIVE

I wake up after a night of bizarro dreams. Cocaine withdrawal is a delightful cornucopia of depression, anxiety, chills, body aches, tremors, shakiness, and exhaustion. I've got all of the above. I'm convinced the only thing that would make me feel better is more coke. But I also know the initial rush of euphoria wouldn't last very long. So I'd go into withdrawal again, needing even more drugs to feel better. The cycle goes on and on and then basically, you die. This I know intellectually. But physically, all I want in my system is that sublime snowy powder.

Nikki enters my room like a punked-out Florence Nightingale, carrying a tray. When she sets it down on the bed, I see a plate of scrambled eggs, toast, orange juice, a vitamin, and a pitcher of water.

"I figure the best way for you to detox is here at home rather than dragging you to some fancy-schmancy clinic. You didn't ingest that much shit so getting it out of your system shouldn't take too long."

"Sounds like a plan." I'm ravenously hungry so I begin eating the eggs, which taste great.

"You need protein to repair your weakened muscles. Drink lots of water, too, to help get the toxins out. And take this multiple vitamin."

I wash the vitamin down with the orange juice. "Mmm."

"It's fresh. I've lived here over thirty years and today's the first time I ever picked oranges from one of my trees. Man, you gotta squeeze a lot of those fuckers to get a glassful."

"Thanks." I'm onto the toast now but have to stop after a few bites because the crunching sound is too loud for my poor head to handle.

"I talked to Dan this morning and he put me in touch with Kira. I convinced her not to press charges."

"Press *charges?*"

"You assaulted her."

"Oh. I did, didn't I?" The memory of yesterday comes back to me like a déjà vu from hell and suddenly the thought of finishing my eggs makes me queasy. I injured Kira who has always been nothing but kind to me. When I was in rehab, she sent me a beautiful antique bisque doll with a card that read, "I know you aren't allowed visitors so I'm sending this friend to keep you company." I don't know if she had anything to do with the joint in my purse, but what made me think I can just go around hurting people based solely on suspicion? Oh yeah, drugs.

"Finish your eggs," Nikki says, interrupting my thoughts.

She's right—I need to eat more to feel better. I want to say something to let her know how much I appreciate everything she's done for me. But all I ever do is thank her and that just brings more attention to my ongoing shame. So I eat in silence with Nikki perched at the edge of the bed watching me like a mother sparrow.

I'm struck by how caring she is, especially when compared to my stage mom who clearly lost any maternal instincts she might have had the moment Hollywood came calling. My dad left us with practically nothing and her job as an assistant manager at Gordman's department store barely paid the bills. So she was more than eager to move to L.A. where she became my manager. Her idea.

I realized my mom was self-centered years ago. My dad had been arrested for DUI and she felt humiliated. She decided not to post bail so he'd have to do time in jail. When he got out, she refused to have sex with him for six months. I know this because she told me so. I was thirteen.

When my mom said goodbye to me a few days ago at the Oakwood, we had an uncomfortable conversation. "Let's hope those rehab idiots know what they're talking about," she said as she handed her luggage to the Uber guy.

"What do you mean?"

"That I'm the villain. It's *me* who's driving you to drugs."

"Don't be dramatic, mom. No one said that."

"I was a damn good manager and you know it. You'll never find one that'll work as hard as I did."

It struck me then that my mom's separation anxiety was about money, not me.

"Well, I hope you do well on your own, Devy," she lied as she stepped into the car. The Uber guy closed the door for her and as he got back into the car, gave me a sympathetic wink.

"I wish I could believe you," I wanted to say. Instead, I told her how much I'll miss her.

I leaned in to kiss her goodbye, but suddenly the window rolled up and we both pulled back. The Uber guy looked mortified. When he realized what he had done, he cried, "Sorry!"

As the car drove away, I broke down crying, right there in the parking lot. And then laughing. The Uber guy was able to say what neither of us could.

• • •

I sleep for a couple hours, then get dressed and come downstairs to find Nikki on the couch with her laptop. When she sees me, she snaps it shut.

"What were you looking at?" I ask.

"Funny things cats do, what else?" She says this in a musical voice and I know instantly she's hiding something from me.

I look around and am once again confronted with how disgusting this house looks. Half-eaten food everywhere, layers of dust covering the furniture. Yesterday I saw two roaches darting across the coffee table.

"When is your maid coming back?" I ask.

"What maid?"

"You said she was on vacation."

"Oh, right. I fired her ass. She really wasn't very good. I need to find another one."

I nod, but suspect she's lying to me. I think she's embarrassed.

She changes the subject. "Can I borrow your car? I thought I'd meet with Dan in person and try and get you your job back."

The events of yesterday creep back into my woozy consciousness again. "Oh, god. I really screwed things up, didn't I?" I join Nikki on the couch.

"We're fighting an uphill battle. But you never know. You wouldn't believe how many chances I was given on *One More Thyme*. You're the star of the show, the reason everyone watches that banshee crap. Replacing the lead is always risky and sometimes it doesn't pay off."

"I hope you're right." I push some of the stuffing back through a hole in the couch fabric.

"Plus there's the curiosity factor—the execs know a lot of creeps tune in just to see if you look like a junkie or not." I make a disgusted face.

"Sad, but true," Nikki says, then, "Wish me luck," as she gets up, grabs my car keys, and heads out.

As miserable as I'm feeling from the withdrawal, I feel worse about what I did yesterday. I've become a nutcase who inflicts pain on innocent people. I like to think of myself as a decent human being. I love kids and animals and old people; I care about the environment and give money to practically every liberal charity there is. But drugs turn me into something repellent. Let me rephrase that. I voluntarily take drugs that turn me into something repellent. I vow to become a better person. Only then will I become a professional actor who people can count on. Nikki's somehow managed to clean up her act, but unfortunately it was too late; her reputation was already destroyed. I refuse to become another Nikki Barnes—an unemployable punch-line to a joke. I need to go to a meeting.

Nikki pulls my car out of the driveway and I stare at her closed laptop. Yep, there it is. Nikki's laptop. Doesn't belong to me. It's private.

I flick it open, breaking, I'm sure, a couple of twelve-step rules in one fell swoop. Ha! So much for striving to be a better person. I pledge I'll forever stop invading people's privacy just as soon as I check out what's on Nikki's screen.

There it is, right on TMZ: me pushing Kira in the director's chair. The video's looped so I get the pleasure of seeing her fall backwards over and over in all its cinematic splendor.

It's pretty obvious I'm the psycho bitch and she's the innocent victim. The look of hurt and surprise on Kira's face is so genuine I feel the urge to cut myself, something I used to do when I was at my worst. Instead, I scroll down and find another clip—this one taken from a different angle, showing the security guards grabbing me.

I close the laptop shut wishing when I open it next all my exploits will have magically vanished from the web. But we all know the Internet is forever and, oh god, I feel like a soccer ball's been kicked in my gut.

I grab a couch cushion and beat the hell out of it. I toss it on the floor and curl up in a ball, crying, in a fit of self-loathing worse than all that have come before. And there have been a lot.

After all my stints in rehab, you'd think I'd have a clue about what to do with my emotions in the absence of those controlled substances that send me spinning out-of-control. I'm reminded of my dad. He'd come home from school in a decent mood, then open the mail and inevitably find another letter from a publisher rejecting one of his short stories or novels. He'd crumple up the letter muttering, "Goddamned morons," and go straight into the kitchen to fix himself a Scotch. And he wouldn't stop drinking until he was totally wasted. Often my mom and I would have dinner alone, with my dad sacked out on the couch.

"Your father's not feeling well tonight," my mom would say, as if I didn't know what was going on. He didn't have the tools to handle pain and rejection, and apparently neither do I. Yep, I definitely need to go to a meeting. Which means I need to pull myself together.

I look in the bathroom mirror at my disheveled appearance and become overwhelmed. There's so much I need to do to look even vaguely "normal." I once complained to my therapist that I hated looking in the mirror. She told me to stop looking in the mirror. Pretty good advice, actually, so I quit gazing at myself for no good reason, and only use the mirror for practical things. Like now. I pick up my brush and tend to the chaos that is my hair.

The doorbell rings. I wait it out, hoping whoever it is will just go away. But it rings again, this time followed by a male voice bellowing, "Hey, Nikki—get your sorry ass out of bed!"

I go downstairs and creep up to the door. Through the peephole I see a clean-cut young man in a white Oxford shirt. He seems harmless enough and something tells me it's okay to let him in.

"Hey. Is Nick around?" he asks.

"Uh, no. She's not here."

"That's weird. She called this morning and told me to stop by." He looks me over, noticing my red eyes and the odd fact that my hair is a snarled mess on one side and quite lovely on the other. "You... okay?" he ventures.

"Yeah. Sort of."

We both stand there a moment, neither of us sure what to say next.

"Hey, did'ja see? Nick's on TMZ again. This time it's actually good. He holds up his phone, showing me the heinous video. "Looks like she helped out a slag actress who went all bitchcakes on the set of some TV show." I don't say anything.

"I'm Pierce," he says. "Who're you?"

"I'm the slag who went bitchcakes, but you can call me Devon."

Pierce winces. "Ouch. Sorry. Yeah, now I see it—I thought you looked kind of familiar." My head hurts and I feel a migraine coming on.

"You wouldn't happen to have an aspirin, would you, Pierce? Nikki doesn't allow any sort of medication in the house."

• • •

Pierce and I are doing lines of coke on the glass dining room table. Turns out he can get me anything I want. "Anything," he stresses. "Any. Thing."

What they say in meetings is true—availability is a key factor in using. You sit in a barber's chair long enough, you eventually get a haircut. When trauma occurs before the availability, the urge multiplies. And if you're in withdrawal, well, the craving for drugs is off-the-charts.

A woman at a meeting once compared being in withdrawal to being on fire. You'll do anything to put an end to the searing pain you're suffering; you have no other choice. You have to put that fire out. This is the way we addicts behave. No—addict is too kind a word for me, I'm a junkie.

Within moments, the fire is out. I feel full of energy, free of anxiety, life is good. I look at Pierce, trying to figure him out. He's obviously a dealer, but with his pressed blue jeans, not a blond hair out of place, he looks more like a Young Republican. He could be eighteen or thirty, I have no idea.

"Um, Pierce. If we could keep this our little secret..."

"Not a word," he assures me. "To Nikki or anyone else for that matter. This didn't happen." Then he picks up my phone from the table and punches in his number. No last name, just "Pierce."

He hands me my phone and heads out the door. "And if you want it to never happen again, you know how to reach me." I watch him get in his car, a black Jaguar with a, for real, Christian fish on the rear bumper.

I'm euphoric. But I look around and Nikki's decaying house is a serious buzz-kill. I decide to clean it. I put my wireless earbuds in for the appropriate soundtrack and decide to start with an old favorite of my mom's and mine—Fiona Apple's frenetic, "Fast As You Can." I wipe down the blinds and open them up, flooding the room with sunshine and a view of the foothills.

I pick up the litter scattered around the living room and den, including the pieces of ceiling stucco. I vacuum, really getting off on the patterns I'm creating in the carpet. I dust. I sweep. I even Windex a few windows.

Still bursting with energy, I scour the kitchen, washing the dirty dishes, wiping down and organizing the lacquered cabinets, even spraying Raid around the baseboards to try and keep the bugs at bay. I mop the floor. Once I get the grime off, the pink and gray of the linoleum really pop and I appreciate their retro funkiness for the first time.

I race upstairs to straighten up Nikki's room. I leave her messy desk alone and just hang up the various piles of clothes on the floor, make her bed and dust her dresser. None of this is a chore—it's the most fun I've had in months. I feel alive.

Before heading downstairs I come to a closed door in the hallway I've passed many times before. Curiosity gets the best of me and I open it up. The room is dark so I turn on a lamp. What I see makes me take a deep breath and turn off my music. It's a child's room from another era. Everything is covered in cobwebs; it's as if nothing has been touched in years. The dusty rose wallpaper is peeling and the many doll faces stare at me, totally creeping me out. The name "Julia" is spelled out in painted wood letters on the wall above the bed.

There's a low dresser that's cluttered with framed photos. They seem to be in chronological order with the first being a birth photo in a pink cloth frame. A much younger-looking Nikki is in a hospital bed, delicately holding her newborn baby with her handsome pony-tailed husband seated at the edge of the bed. This photo's followed by a handful more— Julia in a onesie, at the beach, at the zoo, with Mickey Mouse at Disneyland. She has silky blonde hair and pale blue eyes.

I pick up a large scrapbook and sit down on the pink ruffled bedspread to check it out. Its pages are filled with old photos, again, all in chronological order. Birthday parties, Julia riding a pony, sitting at her rock star daddy's drum set, drumsticks in her tiny hands. There's a photo of Julia and an older woman who might be Nikki's mom—there's a resemblance.

As Julia gets older, her appearance changes drastically. There are dark circles under her eyes, her face void of any baby fat—no cheeks to pinch. The photos remind me of the emaciated kids you see on those unbearable TV ads for organizations that feed starving children.

There are several photos of Julia in a hospital room, lying in bed, usually surrounded by colorful balloons. In one, she's hooked up to a machine with tubes coming out of her nose. I can barely bring myself to look at it.

Soon the pages of photos are replaced with yellowed newspaper clippings. Articles about Julia's illness and Nikki's fundraisers for it. And finally, obituary notices including lengthy ones in the trades.

I put the scrapbook back and move over to a nightstand where I notice a large music box with a ceramic figure of a girl resembling Julia on top. I turn it over and wind it up. The figure slowly pirouettes as tinkly music plays. I recognize the haunting melody as "Julia" because my mom is a huge fan of the Beatles, especially John Lennon. I close my eyes and sing along with the music about Julia, the ocean child who sings a song of love.

I open the box and discover a small plastic bag inside. I pick it up and realize it's filled with ashes and tiny bits of bone. This is all that's left of the delicate little girl in the photos. It strikes me that someday I might be in a plastic bag in some neglected room too. Probably sooner rather than later, the way things are going. I feel a chill.

"Devon! What are you doing in here?"

I gasp. I'm holding Nikki's cremated child in my hands. I quickly place the bag back into the music box and shut it, but the tinkly music continues to play.

"I know I shouldn't be in here, Nikki. I was cleaning. I'm so sorry."

I expect the worst but Nikki doesn't freak. Instead, she sits down on the bed. "It's okay," she says.

"She was a beautiful little girl." I pick up one of the pictures from the dresser and sit down next to Nikki.

"Even more so on the inside. There's not a day goes by that I don't cry for her."

"I guess you never get over something like that, huh?"

Nikki shakes her head. "I did everything in my power to keep her alive, but it wasn't enough. I guess God had other plans for her. If the sadistic bastard even exists."

I don't know what to say. We sit in silence for a moment, the music box having gradually wound down.

"Why are you doing that?" Nikki asks. I don't know what she's talking about.

"Doing what?"

"Tapping your leg like that. You've been doing it since you sat down. You're not even aware of it. You're fucked up again, aren't you?"

"What?" I stall because I don't know what else to do. I try to stop my leg from tapping, but it only makes me tap my fingers instead.

"Don't even try, Devon. Your pupils are bigger than your tits. And normal people don't go on manic cleaning sprees. You're on something."

"I can explain."

"I'm all ears." She crosses her arms against her chest.

I don't know where to begin and can't think clearly. I open my mouth, but nothing comes out. Nikki jumps in.

"Let's start with where the hell you even got the stuff. Did you call a dealer? Did you let a dealer into my home?"

"No. Of course not!" I bite a fingernail, considering what to tell Nikki.

"I saw the TMZ thing today. On your laptop. It really upset me."

"You opened my laptop?"

"Uh-huh."

Her arms are still crossed and her head is turned at an angle. She looks like a stern teacher listening to a student explain why she hasn't turned in her homework assignment.

"That's what started this whole thing. Plus, I was still feeling wack from the withdrawal. Then Pierce showed up."

"Pierce."

"Yeah, your friend. I don't know his last name. He said you called him this morning and asked him to come over."

"I don't know any Pierce."

"He drives a black Jag. Blond hair. Real straight looking."

"I have no idea who you're talking about. You're lying to me." She grabs my chin and turns my head to face hers. "Just tell me where you got the drugs."

"Pierce!" I say louder than before as if that will suddenly make Nikki know who I'm talking about. I pull away from her grip. "We did a few lines of coke. I was having horrendous withdrawal symptoms and was desperate. You know exactly what I was feeling, I know you do."

"You're damn right I do! And I also know addicts are liars. I don't know who the hell Pierce is or how you got your hands on drugs, but I know one thing for sure and that is you are slowly killing yourself. If one of us had some cash I'd get you back into rehab, but the fact is, Devon, you're out of a fucking job."

She gets up and walks out of the room. I follow her down the hallway. "Wait—what?"

"You heard me. I tried my best. I waited an hour just to talk to Dan, then I practically got down on my knees and begged him. He said it wasn't up to him—it was the network. They're worried about losing subscribers."

Nikki goes downstairs and I follow, holding onto the rail, as my knees are weak.

"So, no job and no cash?" I yell at Nikki's back as if it's her fault. She turns around at the bottom of the stairs and looks up at me. She speaks to me calmly, as if I were a child.

"They're direct depositing your last check into your account and giving you a generous severance payment. You don't have to worry about money for a while." She heads toward the kitchen and I follow. "You're welcome to live here as long as you need to, but only if you stay clean. I have very little tolerance for this shit anymore."

Nikki gets me a glass of water from the kitchen sink, practically shoves it at me and says, "drink." I sit in the freshly scrubbed restaurant-style booth, no longer afraid of what might lurk in the seams of the pink naugahyde that I wiped down. I drink the whole glass of water and hand it back to Nikki. As I drink the second glass I can practically feel my skin become more supple.

"The *People* interview and photo shoot are tomorrow morning," Nikki says. "You want me to cancel?"

"No, you go. I do think the article could help others. I'm willing to sacrifice a little of my pride."

"What do you want me to say?"

"We're both working the program. We really only have one choice. The truth. What do you think?"

"I think the kitchen looks groovy without the roaches," she says as she exits the kitchen.

• • •

I spend the rest of the day in bed, suffering the inevitable crash that follows the high. I'm simultaneously exhausted and agitated, a unique state that we addicts know all too well. I can't seem to fall asleep—too restless, and of course, my body is craving cocaine. I'm depressed, too, and toy with the idea of suicide as I usually do when I feel like this, but the thought of killing myself would require a plan and I have no energy to devise one.

Nikki continues to bring me water and occasionally some chocolate candy, which she says used to help her with her withdrawal. We watch TV for a while, but it only makes me more irritable. It's an annoying reminder that I've destroyed my career. I flip through the channels, searching for something that'll make me feel better. I settle on the old Warner Bros. Looney Toons, which actually makes me laugh until Wile E. Coyote shows up and I'm overcome with anger. As if *he* personally killed Wheezer. How messed up is *that*?

# CHAPTER SIX

Another tortuous night of sleep, plagued by nightmares and the sound of thunder and pounding rain. I'm still recovering from the last and most disturbing dream I remember in excruciating detail. I'm Brianna, running across the misty fields of Ireland in the moonlight, being chased by a pack of rabid coyotes—I'm pretty sure there's no such thing as Irish coyotes, but in my dream they're very real. I come upon a Gothic castle and pound on the door. Kira answers, covered in blood from head to toe, like Carrie. She lets me in, as the coyotes snap at my heels. She begins crying, and when I reach out to comfort her, she's a life-size version of the bisque doll she gave me. The doll opens its mouth and wails like a banshee. It takes flight, circling around the enormously high ceiling.

The castle becomes a soundstage. There are cameras, lights, and a crew, although none of them are recognizable to me—they're immobile and have sockets where eyes should be.

Bare-chested Shane is there, doing push-ups and Dan and Tammy from *People* magazine are seated at a table in the middle of the set, inexplicably arranging and rearranging wooden Scrabble tiles to spell out words. Tammy's face is hideously disfigured—more so than in real life, that is—with her eyes where her mouth should be. The tone is one of paranoia. I just want to find a safe place, but everything feels menacing.

Suddenly, I'm inside my house back in Wisconsin, although it doesn't actually look like my house. I find my bedroom. In the center is a large pile of burning books. I choke on the smoke and run out of the room. My mother's in the hallway that's also on fire. She grabs my hand and says, "Come on—we have to get out of here!" We race together, away from the suffocating smoke. As we're running, I realize I'm holding the hand of Nikki, not my mom. You don't have to be Freud to figure that one out. No one can accuse me of having subtle dreams. The hallway seems to go on forever with irritating strobe lights illuminating the way. The smoke is gone, so we stop to catch our breath. "You okay, Devon?" Nikki asks. "I think so. You?" She doesn't answer because she's now Jennifer Thyme, in the form of a cardboard standee. Only her vacant expression has been replaced by a chilling grimace.

I run down the hallway again until I arrive at a cave. A group of paparazzi awaits me, snapping photos with blinding flashes. I plow through them and make my way inside where I see two figures standing in the corner, their backs to me, an adult and a child. I can tell the one on the left is my father. He turns around and smiles at me, and suddenly I no longer feel afraid, despite the fact that he looks the same as the last time I saw him—in his casket. He's dressed in his best suit and tie, and his face has an artificial, rosy complexion, nothing like the jaundiced one he had when he was alive. "So nice to see you again, Devy. I'm very proud of you." He hugs me and his body is surprisingly warm. "Have you met my new friend?" he asks. The small figure next to him has golden hair and is wearing a pale blue dress, reminding me of Alice in Wonderland. She slowly turns around and reveals herself to be a rotting corpse. In her skeletal arms she holds Wheezer who's nothing but mutilated organs and blood-matted fur. I scream and slam awake, my sweaty T-shirt clinging to my body. Whoa. I already dread tomorrow night.

Now that I'm awake, I'm even more exhausted than when I went to sleep. I yawn and look out my window at the rain, relieved to see daylight. If Wheezer were here, I'd grab a book and the two of us would spend the afternoon in bed together.

I'm hungry, so I get out of bed to go downstairs. Beside my closed door on the floor is a tray with breakfast on it. I decide to take it down to the kitchen to eat at the table like a normal person, not some invalid, but the door is locked. I pull hard and can hear something heavy bang against the wood. A padlock? I call out Nikki's name but she doesn't answer.

The adjoining bathroom that leads to the hallway is also locked from the outside. I yell Nikki's name again, this time with a few added profanities, but all I get is silence. Has she actually locked me up like a caged animal? Of course she has and who can blame her.

She probably went out and feared if she didn't lock me in, I'd go out in search of drugs. And who knows, maybe she's right. Or maybe she feared another visit from Pierce—the friendly neighborhood pusher and poster child for Nazi youth.

I look for my phone, but it isn't in my purse where I usually keep it, and in fact, it's nowhere to be found. Now I'm really pissed.

I eat the bagel and cream cheese Nikki left for me, because I'm starving—another symptom of withdrawal—but it doesn't make me feel any better. If such a thing is possible, I'm simultaneously agitated, depressed, anxious, and irritable. I don't know what to do with myself—read, lie down, scream? If I had something sharp I might cut myself, a behavior I quit during my last rehab. I dig my nails into my inner arm, but it feels pointless so I stop.

How could Nikki lock me up? Can I trust her? Is she friend or foe? I pace the floor, my angry footsteps landing harder and harder. Stalking back and forth, I feel like a crazy person. They say if you think you're crazy, you're not. However, with the storm kicking up again and the thunder and lightning crashing and flashing, I feel like a madwoman.

I'm reminded of a scene I once played in *Beverly Hills Banshee* in which I was locked in an attic, and I relive that moment by letting out a primal howl. I'm wailing like a lunatic and it suddenly strikes me as funny. I collapse on the rug and let out laughter that comes from someplace deep inside me. And then the laughter turns to weeping. I miss Wheezer, I miss work, I even miss my mom. Oh, and I hate myself. I curl into a fetal ball and, overcome with exhaustion, fall asleep again.

• • •

It's dusk when Nikki finally unlocks the door. I'm still on the floor, my hair a tangled mess, my long T-shirt reeking of sweat. "Ready to join the living?" she asks, hands on hips.

I sit up. "You locked me in," I say in the most accusatory voice possible.

"You're welcome," she says. I give this some thought. I'm actually feeling better. I'm still exhausted, but the physical craving is gone and that's major. I look up at her, trying to decide how to play this. A part of me wants to yell at her for locking me up. Another part wants her to wrap her arms around me and tell me everything will be all right. I decide to put my feelings on pause for the moment.

"How did the interview go?"

"I'm not sure. You never know what story the..." she makes air quotes, "'writer' has in her own mind before the interview even begins. Tammy Robbins talks a big game about restoring your dignity, the hardships of addiction, blah, blah, blah, but who knows what shitty slant she may put on the article."

"Do you think it will help get me my job back?"

"No. I don't. I think you should just put that out of your mind for now and focus on your health. Go to meetings, get some exercise, stay straight. Then, hopefully the work will come your way."

"You're right. That's what I'll do."

"I should mention, though, that I called your agent today, Marty. I told him you were on the mend and just want to work. I said you'd be down for just about anything—an indie, a web series, a tampon commercial. Am I right?"

"I could sell the hell out of tampons," I say as I stand up with Nikki's help. We're both laughing, and I find myself overcome with gratitude. I hug her and we hold each other for a long moment. She strokes my hair. And then the words, "Thank you," come out of my mouth and make their way into her ear. She stops stroking me. Gently, she pulls away. I watch as she places my phone down on the dresser and walks out.

Detoxing takes time, but it's been over three weeks and each day I feel a little better. I begin my morning by practicing mindfulness meditation I learned online. When I first started, I did it for about five minutes, then ten; now I'm up to twenty minutes. I "follow" my breath as it goes out and goes in. Eventually, my attention leaves the breath and wanders to other places. That's when I return my focus to the breath. I'm not to bother judging myself or obsess over the content of my thoughts. Just come back. Go away and come back. I can already feel the calming effects.

After meditating, I usually spend a couple of hours on the patio reading books from the library, mostly classics from a list my dad once gave me, ranging from Jane Austen to Camus. But I'm also discovering some contemporary literature that resonates with me—Raymond Carver's quietly struggling alcoholics, the emotional violence of Joyce Carol Oates, and Toni Morrison's *Beloved* trilogy. Morrison says the conceptual connection between her three books is the "search for the beloved—the part of the self that is you, and loves you, and is always there for you." I'm on that search. I need to care for myself so that others, like Nikki or my mom, don't have to.

In the afternoons, Nikki and I go to our twelve-step meetings— sometimes we actually walk all the way out of the canyon into West Hollywood and back. Usually we stop for frozen yogurt or if we're feeling decadent, gelato.

Today, before our meeting, we walk to the Canyon Country Store at the bottom of the hill to get the copy of *People* that just came out. We stop at the cart outside the store and get coffee and croissants, which we eat at a picnic table on the front patio. I love this store and not just because my mom and I used to stop here when heading into the valley. It's got a hippie vibe that's hard to resist. Nikki feels the same way.

"Let me give you a history lesson, young lady," she says. "Believe it or not, this general store has been the cultural center of Laurel Canyon for a full century," she says and starts to bring up references to rock n' rollers that are way before my time but familiar to me because of my mom.

"Jim Morrison immortalized the store in his song, 'Love Street'." She sings, off-key, a line about a store where creatures meet. "On this very patio, in the sixties and seventies, dudes used to write songs and jam together. Carole King, Jackson Browne, Linda Ronstadt. You've heard of Brian Wilson?"

"Totally. The Beach Boys."

"How about Graham Nash?" she asks.

"Crosby, Stills, Nash, and Young," I say, proud of myself.

"Excellent! He wrote 'Our House' about this neighborhood." And she sings the chorus. Again, off-key, but not without its charm.

As we walk inside the market and pass the imported candy section, Nikki's still chattering, "Mick Jagger came here for the English Kit Kats and David Bowie bought Flakes, his favorite Cadbury chocolate bar." I pick up one of each so I can tell my mom about it the next time we talk, whenever that may be. We also pass some homemade soaps. I pick one up labeled 'teak and oud' and smell it: mmm.

"This deli counter is unbelievable," Nikki continues, "and there's a wine cellar that used to be a basement apartment where Mama Cass lived."

"Okay, her I don't know. Who's mama was she?"

Nikki laughs. "No, she was part of the Mamas and the Papas."

"Oh! I've heard of them! We sang 'California Dreamin' in my school choir."

"Right, they wrote 'Twelve Thirty'—tell your mom that." She sings its chorus about young girls coming to the canyon. The guy at the checkout counter looks over at us and smiles. I get the sense he hears this kind of talk all the time.

We make our way to the magazine section and find copies of *People*. On the cover is a beautiful photo of Nikki and a much smaller, inset photo of me as Brianna. The headline reads, "Nikki Barnes Dries Banshee's Tears."

We each grab a copy and stand there in the store, reading the article from beginning to end. It's good. The slant is kind of what we suspected and what Tammy alluded to when we first met—the unlikely pairing of a former child star-gone-bad with a current ingénue trying not to go bad. The article is brutally honest and doesn't shy away from my nefarious escapades but it's also upbeat, and for lack of a better word, "inspiration-al." It explores quite a bit of Nikki's past, her ups and downs—mostly downs—and her resilience. She comes across as the foul-mouthed, kooky survivor she is, God love her. I'm hopeful some troubled teen out there who's having his or her own problems with addiction will relate to one of our stories and see that all is not futile.

Nikki can't hide her glee over the article. "This is fuckin' incredible!" she says. Putting myself in her shoes, I can understand why. Her acting career is dead-in-the-water and it must be nice to be getting some atten-tion again, especially the positive kind. And she deserves it, so I'm not at all envious that the article, and cover, gives me short shrift.

I grab a bunch of copies to buy, thinking I'll give them to my friends, then suddenly it hits me: I don't *have* any friends. I burned all my bridges with just about everybody I know, including old pals from Wisconsin who I borrowed money from and never paid back. I consider sending the article to my mom, but there are a few references to her in it that aren't so flattering, portraying her as stage mom and supreme enabler. Whoever did the research deserves a raise—all the details are accurate. Who knows who they must have interviewed to get everything right.

I put the magazines back, except for the one I bring to the counter, while Nikki chats it up with a neighbor she's run into—an aging, ra-ven-haired woman from Morocco who was a pop-star in France many years ago.

The guy at the register is about my age and now that I've got a good look at him, undeniably cute. He's tall and slender, with pale green eyes that look stunning in combination with his black skin. I pay for the magazine and candy, and as he slips them into the bag he casually says, "Good luck to you."

"Thanks." As I turn around he adds, "I confess—I'm a 'fanshee.'" A "fanshee," as you've probably guessed, is the name for fans of my series.

"It started out as a guilty pleasure but I…"

"Whoa, whoa, whoa—wait a minute. *Guilty pleasure?*"

"Busted." He holds out his wrists to be handcuffed. "But hey—you didn't let me finish! Yeah, my friends and I used to make fun of it. I mean, you got to admit, sometimes that shit is over-the-top. But then we realized that's what makes it so cool. And the acting's phenomenal." He waits for my response. "That was a compliment."

"Thank you." I could continue giving him a hard time, but those green eyes have me so transfixed, I'm not sure I can put together an intelligible sentence.

"It sucks that you're leaving the show. It won't be the same without you. I hear Kira Franklin is going to be the new lead. Big mistake. She's a lightweight."

Kira Franklin. My stomach clenches. Maybe Nikki was right about her after all.

"I wish her only the best," I manage to mutter.

He nods his head and grins a goofy grin. I can see he's self-conscious, but he musters up enough confidence to keep talking.

"A lot of celebs come in here and it's no big deal, but I gotta confess I'm a little star-struck right now."

While I'm flattered, I'm also uncomfortable with his praise, given recent events, so I shift the focus with a line of scintillating conversation.

"So, um… how do you like working in the canyon?"

"I love it. But managing the store is just part-time. I'm going for my Masters at UCLA."

Before I have a chance to respond, Nikki plops down about a zillion *People* magazines on the counter and says to green eyes, "Read anything good lately?"

He laughs. "Sure did. Congrats, Nikki—damn, you look hot," he says pointing to one of the covers. "Ooh, I'm not supposed to say that, am I? Kinda rape-y. Forgive me, Lord. What I *meant* to say is they captured you really well."

"Yeah, yeah, yeah," Nikki says. They photoshopped the shit out of me and thank God for that."

After she pays for the magazines and some cigarettes, she grabs a pen and signs her name on the cover of one of the mags, then hands the pen to me to do the same. I'm embarrassed to be giving an unsolicited autograph, but I sign anyway. Nikki gives the magazine to him.

"Here. Sell it on eBay. Make some cash for textbooks, college boy."

He laughs. "Thanks, guys." We turn to leave and he calls out to me.

"By the way, my name's Tremaine. My friends call me Trey."

"Bye, Trey," I say, confirming the new friendship and hoping it lasts.

*PEARL*

# CHAPTER SEVEN

Me and Frank are sitting at the kitchen table. I read the last paragraph out loud from the magazine. "Having Nikki as a 'been there, done that' fairy godmother, Devon O'Keefe's sad story is more than likely to have a happy ending." I look up at Frank.

"It's none of your goddamn business," he says, biting into a bologna sandwich I fixed for him.

"What do you mean, none of my business? Nicole's my *daughter*."

"Yeah, well, she ain't mine." Frank grabs the magazine out of my hands and flings it across the room.

"Why do you read that crap? The past's the past," he says. "Why can't you just let things be? I'm sick of your bitching and moaning." He gets up, throws the paper plate and the crust of his sandwich in the garbage.

"You don't understand. What I have to live with. Everyday."

"I understand plenty."

"No, you don't. You're drunk. And it's not even noon." I grab a few Sociables out of the box and munch on them, my lunch. I don't feel like eating much these days.

"You pickin' a fight with me? Is that what you want? A fight?" Frank walks round the table.

"No," I say, but maybe I do.

"Don't start with me, Pearl." He goes to the cabinet, takes out a bottle of bourbon, pours himself a drink.

"You're a pathetic drunk," I say. "I don't know why I stay with you."

"No one else'll have you, that's why."

I get up and pick up the magazine across the room.

"Give me that rag!" he yells.

"No!"

He comes over and grabs it out of my hands, starts swatting me in the face with it, over and over again.

"Here, you want it?" Swatting me again. "You want it?"

I shove him away, knowing I had went too far. He shoves me back and his shove is strong, not like mine. I stumble backwards, fall hard on the floor. I don't cry. I never cry.

# DEVON

# CHAPTER EIGHT

Dorothy's just clicked her heels three times and is transported back to Kansas. I love this movie but it's always perplexed me. Why the hell does Dorothy say, "There's no place like home" when home is a dismal, black-and-white world compared to the colorful land of Oz where she had an exhilarating adventure? Wisconsin's not the Kansas of the movie and L.A.'s definitely not Oz, but the analogy isn't totally inappropriate. My misadventures in this deceptively golden, enticing land have been fraught with danger, but unlike Dorothy, I believe wholeheartedly there's a man behind the curtain. Things are not what they seem here on the other side of the rainbow, but for now it's the place I call home.

I pause the movie when Nikki pops her head in. It's late morning and I'm still in bed.

"Get dressed. You've got an audition."

"For real?"

"It's a play. A friend of mine is the director—Nigel Aldrich. He saw the *People* article and thought you might be right for the female lead, a young starlet."

"Oh my God!"

"Don't get too excited. It's one of those ninety-nine-seat Equity waiver theatres and you won't make much dough."

"I don't care, I just want to work." I picture myself on a small stage with flimsy flats that shake when an actor closes a door. I also envision an audience that's half full, after all the friends and family of the cast have seen the show opening night.

"Wow. I'm going to become one of those poor souls who pass out flyers to people who don't want them. Yesterday's TV star, today's struggling actor. It all happened so fast."

"No shit. But remember—it's a good opportunity to show you can actually act." She enters the room and looks at me. "You *can* act, can't you?

"What's the play?" I ask.

"*Day of the Locust*. Nigel said it's adapted from a book."

"It is. By Nathanael West. It's one of my favorite novels. My dad turned me on to it. It's about the dark side of Hollywood... how appropriate."

"I thought it was about bugs," Nikki says as she fires up a cigarette.

"The locusts are a metaphor. In the book, people flock to Hollywood to realize the American dream, then become disillusioned and angry when it eludes them."

"What happens to the people?"

"Their disappointment and bitterness create a violence that becomes this sort of apocalyptic nightmare. You should read it—it's powerful."

"*Read* it? I'm *living* it."

I laugh. "What time is the audition?"

"Two-o'clock. It's at a little theatre on Santa Monica."

"I have to figure out what I'm going to wear." I rifle through my closet, passing up outfit after outfit until I come to a white cotton dress with a blue sailor collar. I bought it at a vintage store on Melrose, thinking it might come in handy some day, but have never worn it. I pull it out and hold it against my body. "This is pure Faye Greener. That's the character I'm up for—she's a young woman desperate to become a movie star."

"Desperation. You can play that in your sleep. No offense."

"None taken. Finally, all my pain and suffering of the last few years might pay off."

"Break a leg, kiddo." Nikki says, which is exactly what my mom used to say. She leaves the room and I get dressed. I'm trying not to get too excited so I'm not devastated if I don't get the part. But in my mind I'm already cast and the reviews are stellar.

• • •

East of Highland, while driving on Santa Monica, I wonder what Nathanael West might've made of Hollywood today. My guess is he'd think not much has changed since he wrote his novel. The people waiting on bus-stop benches look as grim and dissatisfied as those in his book. Transvestites with sad painted faces and cheap stilettos linger at a donut shop. Day laborers hang out on the corners, wondering why they came to this country in the first place. A schizophrenic woman argues with her invisible friend. Desperate runaways carry backpacks full of their life's belongings. How is it they can afford all those tats and piercings on their way-too-thin bodies? I don't want to know.

This stretch of the street is called Theatre Row and hand-painted signs advertise plays that few people have ever heard of. I find the Hudson Theatre and manage to find a parking space right in front.

Inside the theatre I sign in and take a seat in the tiny lobby among other young women, all wearing, I should add, vintage dresses. A young woman who looks a little harried hands me some script pages with my character's lines highlighted in yellow.

"Here are your sides. You'll be reading for Faye Greener. When you get in there," her chin points to the direction of the auditorium, "don't make small talk with Nigel. He's got a lot of girls to see and doesn't like being distracted."

"Got it," I say. I look over the pages, as do the other actors. Some of them are reciting the lines out loud to themselves and making exaggerated facial expressions. I don't do this, but focus instead on what the subtext is, something I learned from my acting teacher back in Kenosha. I have time to read the pages over several times before they call my name.

I enter the dark auditorium, and a voice from somewhere tells me to step onto the stage where an actor in his late-twenties shakes my hand and says, "Hi, I'm Matteo Serrano. I'm a huge fan of yours."

"Thanks. Are you reading for the role of Tod Hackett?"

"Yeah, actually I've already been cast."

The director is seated in the middle of the auditorium, but it's difficult for me to see him due to the stage lights. He doesn't introduce himself, just says, "Whenever you're ready, love" in a British accent.

We read the scene and it goes pretty well. Tod Hackett is the leading male role, an artist who's come to Hollywood to work as a set designer for a big studio. In the scene he's trying to seduce me, but my character, who's a bit full of herself, puts him off. At one point, after a dismissive line of mine, I can hear the director let out a snicker. I'm hoping it's a positive reaction to my line reading and not a derisive laugh at my acting ability.

"Yes. Right. One more time, please," the director says.

"Okay. Do you have any notes?"

"No, but I know you can do better." Yikes.

We do the scene again, this time I try to make more eye contact with Matteo and be less beholden to the script. I also experiment with making Faye more theatrical, more artificial as I remember her being in the book. It seems to go better.

"That'll be all, Matteo," the director says.

Matteo shakes my hand again before leaving the stage, whispering, "Nice job—hope you get the part."

The director comes up on stage and I finally get a look at him. He's probably close to thirty, very tall, wearing all black. He has a beard and a thin mouth—sort of severe looking; it wouldn't surprise me if his British accent were fake. He's just that kind of a guy—he strikes me as someone who takes himself way too seriously.

"I'm the director, Nigel Aldrich," he says, stating the obvious. "Let's do the other scene. I'll be reading the role of your father, Harry Greener."

I rifle through my script pages and one flutters to the floor at Nigel's feet. He makes no effort to pick it up, so I do, feeling foolish and clumsy.

I organize the papers and find the appropriate section. This scene is a little more dramatic than the last. My father, a down-and-out vaude-villian clown has a heart condition and is having a coughing spell. I'm concerned, trying to take care of him.

When we finish, there's silence—no "good job" or "thank you." I stand there, feeling self-conscious as the director stares at me. Finally, I say, "Would you like me to read it again?"

"No, that won't be necessary. Have a seat." I find a bentwood chair, pull it over, closer to where he's standing and sit down. He also grabs one and sits down, backwards, cowboy style.

"So, you're an actor after all," he says, looking down at the floor. "I certainly couldn't tell from that rubbish you do on the telly."

"*Did*," I say.

"*Did*," he echoes, finally looking up at me with a faint smile on his face.

"And thank you for the lovely compliment," I say, feeling the need to diss him the way he dissed me.

"You're very welcome." He doesn't continue and I realize this is someone who likes to play mind games—to make conversations as un-comfortable as possible to establish he's the one in control. I decide not to buy into it.

"I love this material," I say. "It's not just dark, it's also witty and satirical. I like how West was able to find humor and humanity in the grotesque."

"Ah, so you've read the book? Back in high school, I presume?"

"No, just on my own. I like to read."

"Oh, you read, do you? What the bloody hell are you doing in Hol-lywood?"

"Auditioning for plays. Trying to salvage my not-so-brilliant career."

"Well, you can stop now, love. You've got the part."

At first I think he's kidding. It takes a second for it to register.

"Really? I've got the part?"

"Don't make me regret it. I suggest you thank me and shake my hand."

"Oh. Okay. Thank you." I hold out my hand and instead of shaking it, he brings it to his lips and kisses it.

"What happened to the hand-shake?" I ask.

"I changed my mind. I'm the director, remember? It's my prerogative." He turns his back on me and walks off the stage.

"I'll try to remember that. Anything else I should know?" I step off the stage and follow him.

"Audrey will give you a copy of the script and the rehearsal schedule. I'll speak to Nikki about your salary. She *is* your manager, yes?"

"Yes."

"You never know with Nikki," he tosses off. This takes me aback—is he saying she's a liar?

"One more thing," I say. "I'm not fishing for compliments or anything, but why did you give me the part?"

"You're a good actor. You're also resilient. You've been through a lot for someone so young, and you've survived. Faye Greener is described in the book as being like a cork."

He exits the auditorium, and I stay to get the script from Audrey, his assistant. Inside my car, I look around to see if anyone's watching me; when I determine they're not, I scream a triumphant, "Way to go, Devon!" My higher power, whatever it is, has apparently decided to give me another chance. I head for an AA meeting so I can properly thank it.

• • •

After the meeting, I drive home and pull my car into the carport. As I get out, I hear someone say, "Ahoy, matey!"

I look up and see our next-door neighbor, Andy Chiu, carrying groceries from his car to his front stoop.

"Oh, my sailor getup. It's for an audition. I don't normally dress like I'm ready to board the Good Ship Lollipop."

"I figured as much."

"My name's Devon, by the way. I'm staying with Nikki for a while. Until I get back on my feet."

"Yes, I know who you are." And there it is. The same thing I said when I first met Nikki. We're both more infamous than famous.

"You doin' okay without your kitty?"

"It's been tough, Andy. Thanks for helping out—I was totally useless." I notice he's got more groceries than he can handle so I walk over and grab a bag from his trunk. "Here, let me give you a hand." We walk to his front door, which is engraved with a carved lotus flower symbol.

"Nikki said a coyote got to your cat, but I don't think that's what happened," he says.

"You don't?" He opens his door, sets his groceries inside, then takes the bag from me. We stand on his front stoop, which is surrounded by rows of bamboo. "I have an outdoor cat, Chimon. Coyotes can't get to him 'cause my yard's completely fenced in. So is Nikki's."

"Right."

"Another thing—I've lived in this canyon for thirty-four years. Coyotes eat everything on their plate, man. They don't leave the good parts."

"What are you saying?"

"I'm saying not everyone in this canyon is a flower child." It takes a moment for my brain to process this.

"You mean someone slaughtered Wheezer on purpose? Why would anyone do that?"

"I have no idea. The Buddhists say, 'Desire is the root cause of all evil.'"

"Desire for *what*?"

"Perhaps we'll never know. In the meantime, you be careful. And if you'd ever like to stop by for tea, just ring my bell."

• • •

I change out of my dress, feeling creeped-out by what Andy's told me. Since Nikki's not home, I decide to visit the country store so I can share my good news with Trey. I walk down the steep hill, trying to make sense of why someone would kill an innocent animal.

Trey's not at the counter this time, he's stocking cereal boxes on a shelf. Only a few customers are in the store so we're able to chat. He looks glad to see me. When I tell him my news, he gives me a hug.

"Congratulations! Bring a poster by and we'll put it up."

"I will. I'm pretty excited. If it does well here, there's a chance they may take it Off-Broadway, which would be really cool."

"That's awesome," he says. "Do you have time for a celebratory drink?"

"Um... the thing is, I don't drink any—"

"I know. Follow me."

He opens the door for me and we step outside to the patio where he gets two Cappuccinos from the guy manning the coffee cart. We sit at a picnic table that looks like it's been painted by Keith Haring. Looking at Trey sitting across from me, my face feels flushed—-he's even more attractive than I remembered. Today he's wearing wire-frame glasses and I can't decide if they're hip, nerdy, or both, but it doesn't really matter— they look great on him.

"You mentioned you're at UCLA. What are you studying?"

He finishes swallowing his coffee before answering. "Law," he says, and now there's foam on his upper lip. I don't say anything because it's just too damned cute.

"What kind of law?"

"Environmental. My mom wants me to go into Criminal Law—she's an Assistant District Attorney—but that's not gonna happen."

"How come?"

"Well, I hope this doesn't sound pretentious, but I think the environment is the most important issue of our time. I want to make sure I'm doing all I can to ensure my children will grow up in a world where they can actually breathe."

"You have *children?*"

"Hypothetical children. You know, *future* children."

I dash my hand over my head with a whoosh, acknowledging my idiocy. He laughs.

"Anyway, that's why I enjoy working in the canyon. I like being close to nature."

And I like being close to Trey. I don't want to leave yet, but I can't think of anything else to say. He picks up on this, jumps right in.

"So how do you like living with Nikki? Must be a trip."

"Oh, it's a trip. She's one wacky gal, don't you think?"

Trey nods, looking vaguely uncomfortable. "The thing with Nikki is..." He stops himself. Then, "I don't really know her that well. We make a lot of deliveries to her house, mansion, whatever you wanna call that ramshackle place, but that's about it."

"Do you think she's a little crazy? I can't tell."

Trey takes another sip of his coffee, gives my question some thought.

"This is Laurel Canyon. I'd say on the cray-cray scale of one to ten, Nikki's about a five, maybe a six."

"And you would be higher or lower than that?"

"Are you kidding? I'm a two. Hope that doesn't scare you off. I'm really dull. I grew up in Burbank."

"You're not dull," I say quietly, looking down at my coffee.

"Hey, you think you might want to go hiking? The Fryman Canyon trail is just up Laurel Canyon. It makes about a three-mile loop and goes through the Tree People center in Coldwater Canyon. It's pretty decent for an urban trail."

"I have a lot of rehearsals, but I'd love to on one of my days off."

"Is today one of your days off?"

"You mean, like, *now?*"

"I mean, like, in ten minutes when I get off. It's almost dusk, my favorite time for a hike. We can take my car."

"Uh, yeah, why not?"

What looks like a rock band enters the store. They're loud and a little rowdy as they head for the liquor section.

"I'll let you get back to work. I'll be waiting outside."

He looks at his watch. "Nine minutes," he says. "You better not ditch me."

• • •

Trey's right. The hike is beautiful even though it's urban and you can see some houses from the vistas. It's not too crowded and the people we pass are friendly; most have dogs. There's a bit of a wind when we get to the higher altitude. Trey notices and takes off his sweater to give to me. Underneath he's wearing an Ezra Collective T-shirt.

"So tell me," he says. "What's it like to be an actress?"

"Well, first of all, I prefer the term 'actor.' 'Actress' sounds pejorative; it suggests what we do is a secondary relationship to men's work."

"That makes sense. Sorry if I offended you. I should probably point out that I prefer African-American to Negro or Colored Person." I let out a laugh—this guy's funny, too, be still my heart.

"Good to know."

"So you didn't answer my question."

"I could tell you what it's like to be an actor and you might even find it marginally interesting, but this hike is so beautiful I feel like I'd spoil it by talking about myself."

"Yeah, but then I'd spoil it by talking about *myself*," he says.

"Then it's pretty obvious what we need to do."

"Both shut the fuck up? Appreciate the sounds of nature?"

"I can't think of anything I'd rather do more."

And that's what we do. For the entire hike. We hear birds and insects, dogs, the wind. We even see a tarantula in our path. Trey points to it and we both stop and crouch down low to get a good look. I'm no fan of spiders, but seeing this beautiful one out in the wilderness isn't scary at all. Trey gets a stick and kind of pokes it off the path and over to the side so no one will step on it. Makes me realize what a bad rap tarantulas get—they're not even poisonous, but because they're big, hairy spiders, people freak out.

It's the best hike I've ever taken—the most spiritually satisfying experience I've had since landing in L.A. We don't even speak when we see the sunset over the San Fernando Valley—just take a seat on a wooden bench and enjoy the view. It's almost like reading alongside another person—you're alone but not. When we finish the hike, we speak again, and exchange phone numbers as we walk to his car in the parking lot.

"Thanks for the great afternoon," I say.

"It *was* pretty amazing, wasn't it?" Trey shakes his head. "Huh. I actually used the word 'amazing.' I usually hate that word 'cause people overuse it. *Cheese dip is amazing! The Bachelor is amazing! Dr. Scholl's gel inserts are amazing!* Seriously?"

I laugh, because he's so right and because I've often thought the exact same thing.

"But I mean it in its truest sense," he says, taking out his phone and bringing up the definition. "'Causing great surprise or wonder.'" His voice is soft. "Yeah, that's it. Wonder. Full of wonder. Wonderful."

• • •

Trey drops me off at home and before I can tell Nikki my good news, she congratulates me—she's already heard it from Nigel.

She gives me a big hug as I enter the den. "I'm so proud of you!"

I notice she's wearing make-up and looks more put together than usual—slacks, not jeans; a blouse, no T-shirt.

"You look nice," I say, but she doesn't respond to the compliment. Instead, she goes on about my audition.

"Nigel said you were brilliant. 'Course the Brits use that word for just about everything, don't they? But from him that's a huge compliment."

"Thanks, Nikki. Don't spend your ten percent all in one place." My joke is flat.

"Don't be ridiculous. I'm not taking commission on your measly salary. But you can be damn sure I will if the show goes to freaking New York."

I plop down on the couch, tired from the hike.

"Hey, I have some good news myself," Nikki says.

"Oh yeah? What?"

"Actually, I take that back. You can see for yourself tomorrow night. On TV," she adds, cryptically. "In the meantime, let's celebrate."

She goes into the kitchen and comes back with a bottle and two

Champagne glasses. "It's Martinelli's sparkling apple cider. I know—it's a poor excuse for Champagne, but a couple of drunks like us can't be choosy." She pours the cider and we clink our glasses together. "Cheers, salud, and l'chaim! May your professional stage debut knock Hollywood on its collective ass." We each take a sip and, as the sweet liquid goes down, I feel that familiar mixture of joy and fear.

• • •

It's the following night, after dinner when I find out about Nikki's big news. We're eating popcorn on the couch in the den, watching a segment she's done for *Entertainment Tonight* on her big screen TV. I guess that explains why she was all made up yesterday.

I'm more than a little surprised. Surprised that she didn't tell me beforehand she was doing it. And surprised that the focus of the piece is on how Nikki has helped me get my life together and stay off drugs.

I didn't mind the *People* article because it did some damage control regarding my meltdown on the *Banshee* set. And it might've motivated some teens to get help for their addictions. But I'd rather not keep publicizing my problems and coming off as some sort of helpless victim who needs caretaking. It's just not the image I want to project. And it's not healthy for me to feel that way.

Nikki tells the interviewer about my getting the role in the play, but the words she uses are, "I just got Devon a part in *Day of the Locust,*" as if my audition had nothing to do with landing me the role. These things get under my skin, but I try not to let it show.

"I'm so happy for you. You still look great on TV." My enthusiasm sounds forced.

It's complicated—the truth is I *am* happy for her. I can see how the attention excites her, brings her out of the depression she's been suffering since her daughter died. But I can't shake the feeling that maybe she's using me.

"Oh, I almost forgot!" Nikki says. "I met a producer at *ET* who suggested you and I do a reality series. I guess we're Hollywood's latest 'odd couple.'"

"Yeah, that's not gonna happen," I say, tossing a piece of popcorn at her. "The last thing I want are cameras in my face as I attempt to stay sober." I find it hard to believe Nikki would even entertain such a horrendously bad idea.

Nikki picks up the piece of popcorn, tosses it in the air and catches it in her mouth. "You're probably right. But I'm really itching to work again. Maybe not acting, but some kind of vehicle where I could make a difference. You know, like maybe a talk show or something where I could help troubled teens."

"This troubled former teen could use your help tonight. Will you run lines with me? Tomorrow's my first rehearsal and I want to be off-book as soon as possible."

"Sure thing." I hand her the script and whatever feelings of resentment I may have had for her vanish. Sometimes I forget Nikki's middle-aged; I think of her as a fun best friend, a contemporary. Other times I can't help but compare her to my mom and she always seems to come out ahead. I think my mom would've pooh-poohed the whole theatre thing I'm doing; she wouldn't have understood why I would want to work for such low pay.

While we're running lines, the phone rings—the land line. I pick it up since it's on the end table next to me.

"Hello?"

"Is this Devon O'Keefe?" The woman's voice sounds elderly and not at all familiar.

"Yes, it is."

"Oh, thank God. Is Nicole around?"

"You mean Nikki? Yeah, hold on a sec."

"No, no!" the woman says with urgency. "It's you I need to talk to. Listen to me, very carefully. This is very import—" Suddenly the line goes dead.

I look at Nikki. "We got disconnected." I hit Menu, then Caller List and call back the number. It rings several times, but no one answers. Nikki asks who it was and I relay the short conversation, including the fact that the caller used the name Nicole.

"Probably some demented fan. It happens from time to time. There's a lot of sick fucks out there. I have no idea how they get my number, but these days anything's possible."

"I guess," I say, but the call freaks me out and I'm having trouble concentrating on the script. "Let's forget running lines for now. I'm gonna take a long bath and go to bed early."

"Good night, Devon. Hope your first rehearsal goes well tomorrow. I'll miss having you around."

"Good night," I say as I start to head up the stairs. I glance back at the phone sitting there on the table and wonder how it is that an inanimate object can look so ominous.

# CHAPTER NINE

I open another bottle of wine and take a few long slugs, then nearly fall over my own feet. Wearing platform shoes isn't easy when you're drunk. I'm at rehearsal and the wine is actually grape juice and I'm not drunk at all, just acting. When the scene's over, Nigel says, "That's the most convincing drunk I've ever seen on stage and I've seen quite a few in my time."

"I've done some research. You may have heard."

"Yes you have, love, yes you have."

It's been a full, rewarding day and I'm jazzed that Nigel seems so pleased with my work. Everything I do is either "lovely" or "brilliant," and the sarcasm he affected at the audition isn't exactly gone but now tinged with affection. He's definitely pretentious, but at least he's talented—not only as a director but also as the writer of the show. It's not an easy novel to adapt to the stage and he's done such inventive things with it.

The cast is great. Most of them have theatre training and some have dabbled in TV. A wonderful character actor who was on a soap for thirty years plays my father, but aside from him, I'm the only "name" in the cast.

One odd thing: Audrey. She's the super-efficient assistant to Nigel who never seems to lose her cool, even when she's the target of his biting barbs. She keeps everything in the production running smoothly, but aside from feeding me dialogue when I call for a line, we've had almost no one-to-one contact.

Today, as I'm going over my lines during a break, she joins me on stage carrying a bag of Funions. "Want some?" She digs inside and holds out a handful of them.

"I'm good."

She pops them in her mouth, making loud crunching noises.

"I've been so crazy-busy," she says, her mouth full, "we haven't even had a chance to get to know each other. Maybe we can grab a drink some-time after rehearsal? Oops, forgot. You don't drink. I do. Like a fish!" She grabs some more Funions, stuffs them in her mouth. "Coffee then?"

"Coffee it is." I can't tell yet if I find her funny or obnoxious—it could go either way.

"You know, we've worked together before. On *Banshee*. You know the scene they shot at the Beverly Center? I was in the crowd, right up front. The director even gave me a line." She yells it right in my face: "Hey, no pushing!"

That decides it. Obnoxious.

"We also have a friend in common—Kira. She let me hang out on the set sometimes. Oops, another faux pas. Sorry. I know you have some issues with her."

"Kira's great," I say, a trace of anger in my voice. I think she picks up on it. Maybe she's not as clueless as she appears.

"I'll let you go," she says, crumpling the now empty bag of Funions. "I need to study my lines too—I just haven't had the time."

"Oh, are you in a show?"

"Sort of." She laughs. "I'm your understudy."

Good to know.

• • •

Rehearsal's over. Nigel chastises a few of the actors who aren't off-book yet. "I don't want to see any scripts here tomorrow, capiche?" he says. "We open in two weeks, people, if you need reminding."

I gather my things, humming Ella Fitzgerald's "A-Tisket, A-Tasket," which Nigel's been playing all rehearsal long. As I step outside, my humming comes to an abrupt stop when an oblivious walking/texting teen bumps into me, reminding me it's no longer 1939. I'm about to get in my car when a middle-aged tourist stops to ask directions.

"I think we're turned around," the man says. "Where's Madame Tussaud's Wax Museum? My wife wants to see George Clooney."

Clearly he's wandered too far from the hub of Hollywood and Vine. As I'm giving him directions, a dead-eyed male hustler rubs his crotch as he passes us, trying to catch the attention of the tourist whose family stands nearby, looking at a map.

"Dicey neighborhood, huh?" the man says.

"There are worse."

"Thanks for the directions, young lady. You be careful now." He rejoins his family, and they head north toward Sunset.

As I open my car door, I hear Matteo call out my name.

"Hey, Dev. My boyfriend's band is playing at the Viper Room tonight and I'm trying to get a bunch of people there to support him. Wanna come?"

"The Viper Room? You mean the nightclub where I'll be surrounded by real booze and those who drink it?" I ask, smiling.

"Oh. Right. Sorry." He scratches his head and looks incredibly awkward.

"Don't be. Actually, I'm feeling pretty good about my sobriety at the moment. I think I can handle it, in fact, it might even be good for me."

"Some of the cast and crew will be there, but feel free to invite anyone you'd like." Trey pops instantly in my head and I'm excited at the possibility that he'll be free to join us.

"What's his name?" Matteo asks.

"Whose name?"

"The guy who's making you smile just thinking about him."

"Am I smiling?"

"See, you don't even know it. Must be serious."

"Naw, it's just a crush. I'm not ready to be in a relationship. But, for the record, his name is Trey."

"Trey. Tres interesting."

"Oui. There. That's all the French I know."

"Au revoir, then," Matteo says as he heads for his car. "Déjà vu, hors d'oeuvres, and merci beaucoup."

"De nada."

• • •

"The Viper Room on Sunset, just east of San Vicente. Oh, and it's not a date."

Trey brings a hand to his chin and strokes it, looking intentionally professorial. We're standing in the middle of the country store; I've stopped here on my way home from rehearsal. Trey looks around and finds there's no one in the store.

"Just curious. Why is it not a date? Not that I was assuming it was, or anything."

"Because dating someone before you work your fourth step is like wearing a hot new outfit with dirty underwear."

"Interesting metaphor. What does the program say about *this?*" He takes my head in his hands and kisses me gently on the lips. I pull away, not because I want to but because I have to.

"That would be a definite 'no.'" I move away and sit on a stack of wine cartons.

"That's cool. I can wait."

It's starting to dawn on me how stupid I was to begin a friendship with someone I'm attracted to at this point. Someone kind. Someone I could easily hurt. It frightens me.

"Trey—you know very little about me. If you knew the real me, there's no chance we'd be having this clandestine little..."

"I know a lot about you." He sits on some boxes across from me.

"You think *People* or the Internet tell you who I really am? Or maybe you're just attracted to Brianna. Is that it? Are you looking forward to hearing me wail like a banshee when we're in bed?" Totally uncalled for, I know, but I can't help myself. I lash out when I'm scared.

"You're putting words in my mouth. Calm down."

"FYI, women do not like to be told to calm down. It actually has the opposite effect."

"Sorry. It's just, this conversation has taken an ugly turn and I'm not sure why."

I stand up. "Because I'm an alcoholic and a junkie, that's why. I've stolen, I've lied, I even struck my own mother in the face." I roll up the sleeves of my blouse and thrust my scarred inner arms at him.

"See these? I used to cut myself. On purpose. To feel alive. Is that the kind of girlfriend you want?"

Trey doesn't answer, just rubs his hand over his face.

"What kind of sick man wants to get involved with someone like me? Are you so star-struck you're willing to overlook—"

"Hey, what's with the fucking insults!" Now he's standing. "Did it ever occur to you that I'm capable of seeing the good in people? That maybe I believe in you and could help you piece your life back together again?"

"Oh, now I get it, a rescuer. Yeah, that's a healthy dynamic for a relationship."

Trey lets out a sigh. "Look, whatever I say is going to piss you off, so why don't we just end this conversation before one of us says something hurtful."

"Too late for that," I mumble as I storm out, wondering if I have time for a meeting to help deal with my off-the-charts self-loathing.

• • •

I use my sleeve to wipe away tears as I drive up the hill from the store to Nikki's house. A black Jaguar is ahead of me. It's Pierce's car—there's a Christian fish symbol on the bumper. Someone is next to him in the passenger's seat and as I get closer I think it might be Nikki. I'm so discombobulated I nearly swerve off the road.

I keep following them, but slow down to create some distance. The Jag pulls up to the curb near Nikki's carport and the driver turns off the motor. I park my car where I am and get out, sneaking up the street from tree to tree like I'm in some cheesy woman-in-peril Lifetime movie. Partially hidden by a hedge in front of someone's property, I'm close enough to see them clearly.

The passenger is definitely Nikki—I can see her profile as she talks and laughs. Pierce lights up a joint and passes it to Nikki who takes a toke. I can't believe what I'm watching and wish there were such thing as a remote control that could switch to another channel. They pass the joint back and forth for a while, then I see Nikki's head go down over Pierce's lap. He leans his head back in pleasure. I've seen more than enough. I sneak back into my car and wait there for a while, shaking.

A few minutes later, Nikki emerges from the car and heads inside her house. Pierce makes a sloppy three-point turn in the narrow canyon street and heads back down the hill, his Jag racing at a speed far too fast for these winding roads. I duck down as he drives past my car and decide to leave it where it is, and hike up the hill past Nikki's house to where Andy Chiu lives.

I ring the doorbell and a moment later he opens the door. He's dressed in his usual garb—pajama-style pants and a loose gauzy Nehru-collar shirt. Nikki says he's in his late sixties, but he has the body of a thirty-year-old, slim and muscular.

"I would love to have tea with you," I manage to say. "If you're not too busy." One look at me and he can tell I'm in trouble.

"Come in, come in," he says.

• • •

Andy's place looks more like an opium den—not that I've ever seen one—than a Hollywood Hills home. He lets me check out his sprawling living room with its gem-colored Persian carpets and walls lined with hundreds of books. I skim the spines—Taoism, Chinese herbal medicine, Tantric Yoga.

I perk up when I discover a whole section of Yeats's work adjacent to books on spiritualism, mysticism, and paranormal research—subjects the poet found intriguing. I come upon his *Fairy and Folk Tales of the Irish Peasantry* and take the leather-bound book down from the shelf. My dad was a Yeats devotee; they had something in common after all, both Irish, both writers, both users—alcohol for my dad, weed for Yeats.

I browse the book until I come to the tale of the banshee and am reminded how proud my dad would be that his and Yeats's mutual interest, occultism, would one day define his freckle-faced daughter, in the form of acting a banshee from Irish mythology. I check the copyright page and find it's an 1888 first edition. I carefully place the book back in its place and continue exploring.

I'd feel like I was in the nineteenth century if it weren't for an anachronistic Rolling Stone on a coffee table. And then there's a photo gallery that displays Andy with rapper DMX, and a bunch of actors like Heather Locklear and Gary Busey. It's a little disappointing that Andy displays these photos so blatantly, then I remember this isn't just his home, it's his business, how he makes a living. Actually, I don't really know exactly what he does.

"What exactly do you do, Andy?"

"I'm a healer and life coach." He notices the blank expression on my face. "I practice Far Eastern techniques and alternative medicine to help my clients overcome everything from drug abuse to PMS."

"What kind of techniques?"

"Reiki, acupuncture, Tai Chi, you name it. Would you like a free sample?"

I say yes instantly although I have no idea what he has in mind.

Andy leads me through a doorway draped in exotic-looking fabric and hanging beads to a smaller room filled with glowing candles, the pungent smell of incense and calming Far Eastern music. He has me lie on my stomach on a comfortable cushion, and asks me to lift up the back of my blouse so he can apply an herbal ointment to my bare skin. It smells like sesame oil and feels soothing.

"It's called 'Gua sha,'" he says. "Been around for two thousand years." He picks up a spoon-like porcelain tool and begins scraping my back, hard. It's not unpleasant, but it's just this side of painful.

"Gua sha brings out the impurities in the body. It releases unhealthy elements and stimulates blood flow and healing."

"Is there scientific proof that this actually works?"

"I respect science and wish our leaders did too. But little research from the medical community has been done on some of the ancient techniques I practice. I still believe in them though. I hope science will some day prove them to be beneficial."

"I only ask because I'm struggling to accept things I can't see. Like a higher power."

"Like many Buddhists, I'm an atheist," Andy says, his strokes lengthening to include every inch of my back. "But I too have worked the program and found that my higher power is the Buddha-nature within myself. I turn my will over to this inner Buddha. So far, he's been a mensch." Andy applies more oil to my back and continues scraping. "You may see bruising and red blotches where there's blocked energy, but don't be concerned. They'll soon go away."

"Does that spoon scrape away guilt too? And loneliness?"

"Anything's possible. The life force 'ch'i' is really blocked. Have you been under a lot of stress lately?"

I let out a laugh. "Yes, Andy, you could say I've been under a lot of stress lately. I am seriously stressed."

Andy stops scraping and says, "My agent always asks me 'did you know stressed is desserts spelled backwards?'"

"You have an agent?"

"CAA."

"Really? They used to rep me. Before I ruined my career."

"My pop psychology buddies call that 'catastrophizing.' A career is like a mountain with its peaks and canyons. A mountain cannot be ruined."

I realize I'm in a canyon, both figuratively and literally. I have no idea what to do with that so I just close my eyes and try to envision my life force become unblocked. A graphic from my high school health class enters my mind of an artery that's clogged with plaque. I picture my life force flowing like blood through one of those arteries. Most of it courses through with no problem, but there are still areas where the plaque succeeds in blocking the stream of blood. This is just my first session with Andy; maybe a few more will do the trick.

When he's done, I pull my blouse back down and sit up. "Talk to me," he says. I break down and tell him my entire story—my addiction, seeing Nikki with Pierce, the whole deal. He listens without interruption. When I'm done he speaks quietly but with conviction. "You must talk to Nikki, otherwise you'll be living in an atmosphere of suspicion. That's not healthy. And you must trust your own instincts, Devon. Be sure to always listen to that small voice inside of you. It's rarely wrong."

"You're right. I'll talk to her. But I don't want to leave yet. Your home is so tranquil." I wonder what it would have been like to have someone like Andy for a father—a person who's not volatile or tortured.

"You don't have to leave, my friend. Follow me." He leads me into a dark room and gestures. "Have a seat." I sit on a comfortable couch that faces a large screen TV. Andy leaves the room and comes back in a few minutes. "This is my favorite way to relax," he says, handing me a large bowl. He clicks the TV on. Popcorn and Judge Judy. I love this man.

• • •

Armed with Andy's words in my head, and feeling sufficiently gua sha'd, I go home to talk to Nikki. Funny how I use the word "home" when referring to her house. It's nothing like what I had in mind when I dreamed of moving to L.A. but I remind myself if it weren't for Nikki I'd probably be living on the street. If you screw things up as badly as I have, even white privilege doesn't help.

Nikki's upstairs, so I grab the landline and do a caller ID to reach the desperate-sounding woman who tried to speak with me. It rings for a long time but nobody answers. I hang up and sit on the couch, preparing myself for the difficult conversation I need to have.

Nikki comes downstairs and bombards me with words before I have a chance to talk to her about Pierce.

"Guess what? I got a job!" She's barely able to contain her excitement.

"You're kidding. Doing what?"

"Well, it's not a *job*-job, like I'm not flipping burgers at In-N-Out or anything. I'll be hosting a daily radio show and podcast. I'll be dealing with issues related to troubled teens—you know, sex, drugs, eating disorders—all the things I'm an expert in."

"Looks like *People* and *ET* really paid off."

"Yeah, I can thank you for that." She stands there, waiting for a response. I can't bring myself to say, "You're welcome," in fact I realize I can't engage with her on any level until I get certain things out of the way first.

"I need to talk to you about something."

"Uh-oh," she says. "I don't like the tone of that one bit." She joins me on the couch. "What's on your mind?"

"Pierce. I saw you in the car with him. Why'd you lie to me?"

"Shit."

I wait for an explanation, but she just sits there. I suspect she's stalling, trying to come up with something to dig her way out of the hole she's in. She grabs her favorite throw pillow—Liza Minnelli in needlepoint by Jonathan Adler, and clutches it to her chest. Finally, she speaks. "I'm so sorry. Yes, I lied to you. I *do* know Pierce—and yeah, he's a dealer."

"Okay."

"I didn't want to admit to you that I still take drugs. He supplies me with them." Long pause. "I've been lying about my sobriety."

I don't know what to say. I can't even look at her.

"God, I feel totally humiliated," she says.

"You mean you go to meetings and you're still using?"

"I'm not proud of it. And it's just Adderall, sometimes a little pot, but nothing else, not even alcohol. I didn't want you to know because I'm trying to be a role model for you."

"So is Pierce like your boyfriend?"

"Oh, God no. He's a born again Christian and he's what, like *twelve?*"

"He's a *Christian?* So that fish on his license plate is for real?" This is getting weirder by the moment.

Nikki nods.

"But... I saw you in the car and you were... you know, doing stuff."

"Oh God. You saw that?"

"Uh-huh."

"What can I say? Drugs are expensive. I do what I have to do to get them for free."

"Nikki!" I'm so disgusted I can barely look at her. "Maybe it's time for me to move out."

"Devon, no. Listen—nothing else has changed. I thought you liked it here." She gets up, grabs her cigarettes, and lights one.

"I do. But I feel like I've been living with a stranger. You're not who I thought you were and it creeps me out. And by the way, I hate it when you smoke in the house. I mean, it's your home and I'm a guest, but the second-hand smoke really bugs me."

Nikki immediately finds an ashtray on the corner table and puts her cigarette out in a series of short, angry jabs.

"I'm sorry. I'll try and be more considerate."

Nikki returns to the couch and we sit in uncomfortable silence for a long time.

"When are you getting your other car back?" I ask.

"My car?"

"You said it was in the shop."

"It's a piece of junk. It needed too much work to get it up and running so I sold it to my mechanic for parts. Why do you ask?"

I just shake my head. Clearly it's yet another lie. It's disconcerting how good she is at lying, how quick her responses are, and how convincing she is. More uncomfortable silence.

"Look, I'm sorry," she says as she takes my hand in hers. "About everything. I really care about you and I hate that you feel betrayed—that's the last thing I wanted to do. Give me one more chance to get my act together. I'll stop seeing Pierce, I'll fess up at a meeting, stop the Adderall, whatever it takes to win back your trust." Then she says something that hits me where I live. "You, of all people, know how important a second chance is." I can't argue with that. I've done my fair share of lying and betraying others. I've been given second and third and fourth chances.

"Okay," I say. "Let's just put this behind us." Nikki gives me a hug and for the first time it just doesn't feel right; she reeks of pot and Pierce's overpowering cologne. I feel like I'm going to throw up and can't wait until she releases me.

"Thank you. You won't regret it."

"I'm going to take a shower. I'm heading out later to the Viper Room with some of the cast."

"Yeah, Nigel invited me."

"Oh. So you're going?"

"What—you didn't think I'd let you go to that den of iniquity by yourself, did you?"

"Actually, I don't know what you'd do, Nikki. In fact, I guess I don't know much about you after all, do I?" She looks hurt, doesn't say anything. It's official—I've just alienated the only person in my life who gives a rat's ass about me. I should probably apologize, but instead I head upstairs to take a shower, without looking back.

• • •

In the bathroom, I see Nikki's left her phone on the sink. I turn on the shower and sit on the closed toilet seat. Once again, I become the Queen Invader of Privacy, perusing her texts, photos, and e-mails. I don't even know what I'm looking for, but I'm beginning to fear there are two Nikki's—the loving, nurturing woman who's saved my ass over and over again, and the deceitful nut-case whose behavior I can't even begin to understand but want to.

I'm about to put the phone back when I notice there's video in her photo section. I hit "play" and discover the TMZ footage, or at least the first part of it, up until the guards stepped in. It was obviously shot with a zoom lens by Nikki before she stepped onto the set. Who knows who shot the second part—could've been anyone on the crew. Maybe Kira. Maybe Audrey.

I toss the phone on the sink counter as if it were contaminated. I need to get out of this house as soon as possible. Rather than confront Nikki now, I decide it's best to just find a new place to live. Tonight at the Viper Room I can talk to the cast and crew about that. All I need is a couch.

I'm about to step in the shower when I realize I need to lock the door first. If you've ever seen *Psycho*, you know what's on my mind. I may be gullible, but I'm not winding up slaughtered in the shower like poor Janet Leigh.

# CHAPTER TEN

The Viper Room is a notorious nightclub on Sunset Strip that used to be owned by Johnny Depp. It features live bands—heavy metal, punk, and alternative. Nikki and I just got here; the bouncer, who looks like a Marine, if Marines grew ZZ Top beards, recognizes us. "You ladies better behave yourselves now. We don't want any trouble here, understood?" I'm offended, but Nikki shamelessly flirts with the guy.

"We'll be good, sir, promise. But before we go in can I just do this?" She squeezes his left bicep. "You work out or did you get this from playing badminton?"

He tries to remain Mr. Tough Guy but the slightest of smiles appears on his face. "Badminton," he says. "Good one."

Nikki and I go downstairs to an area near the bar where Nigel, Audrey, Matteo, and a few crew members are seated in a large corner booth. Live music blares from upstairs; sounds like heavy metal, not my fave. Matteo's boyfriend's band, Corpuscle, doesn't go on for another half-hour. Audrey's been here a while and is more than a little drunk.

"My mom was here on Halloween, the night it happened," she says. Her speech is slurred and she's shouting to be heard over the music. I have no idea what she's talking about; no one does. But she continues.

"Her boyfriend comes up to her and goes, 'Hey, you gotta see this. River Phoenix is like having a seizure on the sidewalk.'"

"Who's River Phoenix?" asks the lighting designer.

"An actor, for God's sake!" Nigel says.

"*Stand by Me, My Own Private Idaho...*" Nikki adds.

"He's Joaquin's bro—everybody knows that," Audrey says. She takes a sip from her drink and continues with her story.

"So anyway, they go outside and there he is on the ground, hurling all over the place and rolling around in it and shit. And then, you know... he like, croaks. Right there on the sidewalk. He ODed on cocaine and morphine."

"He was my age when he died, twenty-three," I say.

"So sad," Matteo says. Everyone nods as the conversation comes to a complete halt. My phone vibrates. I look down and see a text from Trey: "im here where r u?" I figure he's either a glutton for punishment, a wuss, or he really does care for me. I opt for number three and decide if he's willing to take things slow and be content with just being friends then maybe there's a chance I could care for him without doing him harm. With what I've just discovered about Nikki, I could sure use a friend.

I text back, "downstairs," and in a minute he shows up. "This is Tremaine, everybody" I shout. Everyone says hi and as he sits down next to me I whisper, "I'm sorry."

"Me too," he says.

"Let me get some drinks," says Nikki. Trey takes out a few dollars and asks Nikki for a Perrier. I suspect the non-alcoholic drink is on account of me and he scores another point.

I ask Nikki to bring me a cranberry juice and club soda. "Ooh, that sounds good," says Nikki, then, "Not much of a buzz, but it's great for bladder infections."

"To no more bladder infections!" Nigel says as he hoists his ale.

Nikki heads for the bar and Audrey follows. "I'll come with you. I need another Manhattan."

Matteo steals a glance at me and does a quick double "thumbs up," referring to Trey. I'm glad he likes what he sees—I do too. Trey sticks out like a sore thumb in this crowd of hipsters and posers, wearing an old stretched-out wool sweater and cargo pants, but that only makes me like him more.

"I need to talk to you about something really important," I say in his ear. "About Nikki. But not here—it's too loud."

"Okay," he says. "Maybe we can sneak outside during the break. You look a little preoccupied."

"I am. But I'm glad you're here." He smiles and puts his hand on my hand, just for a moment. And in that moment, everyone else in the club seems to vanish. It's just me and him.

Nikki and Audrey return with the drinks. Nigel holds court, telling theatre stories and name-dropping like crazy. He loves being the center of attention and, while I admit he's both smart and wickedly witty, I grow tired of him quickly—he's always "on" and never reveals anything real about himself. As my mom used to say, "There's no 'there' there." Apparently, Trey feels the same way. He leans over and says, "Is it me, or is that guy a dick?" I nearly spit out my cranberry juice.

When it's time for Matteo's boyfriend's band to perform, we all move upstairs to the crowded main room. Trey asks, "You want to slip outside now?"

"Let's wait until after the set."

Corpuscle takes the stage. They're a "progressive heavy electro rock" band according to Matteo, who points out his boyfriend, the synth player. They launch into their first song, a trippy tune that gets the crowd going. Some people start dancing, including Nikki and Nigel, but Trey and I hang back and people-watch.

The music is super loud and my body vibrates with the chords. Each beat on the drum is like a jolt of happiness, each guitar strum fills me with joy—no, that's too weak a word. What I feel is euphoria, actual euphoria! I'm blown away at the wonder of that—how can music be so *fantastic*? It's glorious and rich and velvety—coming at me in waves of turquoise and indigo.

I take Trey's hand. He smiles at me and I'm elated. Elated to be near him, to gaze at his beautiful face! I can't get enough of him and my body starts tingling, really tingling, from my toes on up to my neck. I'm swaying to the music, the percussion pounding my soul. The tingling continues but now it's unpleasant—too much sensation. I'm suddenly nauseated and look around to see where the bathrooms are in case I need to retch. But the nausea goes away as fast as it came. No. It's back; it comes and goes like the waves of the ocean.

Now I'm hot, burning—maybe it's the flu? I let go of Trey's hand so he doesn't feel how sweaty I am. I'm perspiring all over, wringing wet, and even more anxious. Something's wrong. Something's wrong with my body. My mouth is dry and my heart is pounding, pounding, pounding, or is it just the drums I'm feeling? Blood speeds, races through my veins and now I'm shaking. I look at my wrists and find the veins moving quickly like dozens of busy highways. Trey asks if I'm okay and puts his hand on my shoulder. It sears through my skin like a hot poker.

"Whoa!" I say. "Something's wrong. I feel... I don't know, the music. It's too much. I can't stand it—I feel trapped. I think I need to..."

"What?" he says. "Tell me what you want, Devon."

But I don't know what I want. The music suddenly slows down, way down, but it's still too loud and it's lost its melody. It's a record being played on the wrong speed, the soundtrack to a bad dream. I fall to my knees and cover my ears.

Trey squats down and yells above the noise, "What's going on? Are you on something? You can tell me," but I can't answer—opening my mouth would take too much effort—I think my lips are glued shut.

"I'm getting Nikki," Trey says and quickly leaves. I stand up and find the crowd has become one large mass, an undulating body like a giant sea creature from the depths of a black ocean. The movement brings on the nausea again, so I close my eyes and see a universe of millions of various-sized dots and gleaming stars, all in Day-Glo colors shooting through my head.

Nikki suddenly appears; I think it's Nikki—she looks different—her face is rubbery. She takes my face in her burning hands and looks into my eyes.

"Oh my god, she's on something," she says. "Devon—what did you take? Tell me—what the fuck did you take?"

"Where's Trey?" I ask. My mouth is working again, but feels thick and sticky.

"He's right there," she says. "Why? Did he give you something? What did he give you? Shit, I *knew* I shouldn't have let you out of my sight."

I look around but can't find Trey. I start to search for him, calling out his name, making my way through the crowded room. But everyone blends together; it's hard to distinguish one body from another. Nikki follows me. "Devon, stop! Let's get you out of here. You need to go to the hospital." I turn back to Nikki and her face suddenly morphs into a scaly reptile that juts out at me, a lizard-like tongue slithering in her mouth. Then, in an instant, she's normal again. Terrified, I scream and step away from her.

I lose myself in the crowd, which is now filled with partially naked people. What is going on here? People turn to look at me; their tongues dart in and out of their mouths. I can't look at them; they make me dizzy, frightened. I spot an exit sign and try to worm my way toward it. Nikki, Nigel, and Matteo follow me, pull at my limbs, tearing my clothes like vicious animals. I fight them off, slapping at them, growling, "Stay away! Leave me alone!"

"Easy now, easy, love," Nigel says, but I can't trust him. I can't trust any of them. He wraps his arms around me, leading me to the exit. Now Trey is on the other side of me, trying to drape his arm around my shoulder. But can I trust him? Isn't he just like all the rest of these monsters? I pull away from them, but stumble onto the floor, which is now filled with wriggling vipers, their large, hinged fangs open and ready. I scream and scramble to stand up, but my balance is insanely off and I'm back on the cold concrete floor. Everyone is staring at me—they look normal now, but I expect them to morph into beasts at any moment. "It's Devon O'Keefe" somebody says and I hear my name echo around the room, but is that who I really am? I don't think so.

Nikki says, "I'm calling 911." A security guard grabs me hard, digging his fingers into my arms and yanks me to my feet. I lower my head and bite his hand as hard as I can.

"Son of a bitch!" I hear, and I'm thrilled that I've broken free! The exit sign is closer now—its red letters pulsing, growing larger, then shrinking, then larger again. I reach the door and thrust it open. I run out into the night and don't stop.

I hear, "Look out!" and I'm bombarded with neon, the sound of horns, and lights of a trillion colors, swirling in beautiful patterns. And then a deafening screech followed by a blow to my body unlike anything I've ever felt. I take flight—I'm airborne, an angel in the City of Angels.

# CHAPTER ELEVEN

"You're a very lucky woman. Not many people survive a significant collision like you did—on Sunset Boulevard, no less." A bearded doctor looks down on me. My brain is as fuzzy as a newborn kitten, but I can tell I'm in a hospital.

"Oh god. Was I driving? Please tell me I didn't kill anyone."

"You weren't driving—you were the pedestrian. The driver of the vehicle is fine. You don't remember the accident?"

"No."

"Loss of short-term memory is common with concussions such as yours. No worries—it usually comes back within a couple of weeks."

I look to my left and see Nikki's seated in a chair next to my bed. She takes my hand in hers and smiles at me. My face hurts too much to smile back, so I squeeze her hand to let her know how much it means to me that she's here.

"The good news is you have no brain damage—just the concussion."

I nod.

"You want the full laundry list?" the doctor asks, as he puts on his glasses.

"Please."

He reads from his clipboard: "No spinal injuries, just a pelvic fracture, broken bones in the left leg..."

I notice the cast and bandages all over my body.

"Torn and sprained ligaments in both legs, and multiple fractures to hips and knees. Lacerations, contusions, and abrasions on face and hands, but I'm not too concerned about those. I don't see anything that will cause permanent scarring or require plastic surgery."

"You said 'the good news.' What's the bad?" I ask.

"Well, it's not exactly bad, just something that needs some attention." The doctor sits on the edge of my bed. "Your urine test revealed you had an exceedingly high level of LSD in your system. Over four hundred micrograms. That's what, I surmise, caused you to run into the street outside the nightclub. I'm suggesting you get drug counseling and rehab once your physical injuries are on the mend. And given your history of alcohol abuse I'd like to order a liver biopsy so we can begin to..."

"How do you know that?"

"The alcohol abuse?" He purses his lips while he carefully chooses his words. He looks directly at me. "The better question would be 'how do I *not* know?'"

"Touché."

"I'll be by tomorrow to check up on you. And when you're feeling better I'll be needing your signature."

"My *signature?* For what?"

"My daughter's a fanshee. You'll be making a fifteen-year-old very happy."

Great. My doctor wants to give the autograph of a serial substance abuser with a bum liver to daddy's little girl. This is Cedars Sinai—he can't find a more appropriate celebrity role model in any of these beds?

• • •

I've been here about a week. Thank god I still have insurance from working on *Banshee*. Nikki has been at my side the whole time—she sleeps on the couch in my spacious private room and only goes home every few days to shower and change clothes. She's been consulting with the doctors and nurses, making sure I'm as comfortable as can be.

My mom came for a couple of days but I was so out of it, I only remember bits and pieces of her visit. She said she had to get back to Wisconsin because of her job, but I later learned from Ricardo, one of the gossipy nurses, that she's got a new boyfriend back there—her boss. She's now an office manager at a real estate company, a position I'm sure she feels is beneath her, having tasted the high life of Hollywood. Before she left, she and I gave the okay to have Nikki be my advocate in the event I'm unable to make my own decisions about my healthcare.

We also decided, because I'm suffering a lot of pain, that it's okay for me to be treated with painkillers. A morphine drip now, then Percocet for when I go home. It was a tough decision to make and I don't feel totally comfortable with it, but Nikki and the doctors will be vigilant so as not to create any new addiction.

The police surmise the LSD was slipped into my cranberry drink in liquid form. They've questioned people who were at the Viper that night including Nikki, Trey, Nigel, Matteo, Audrey, and the bartenders.

It's pretty difficult, if not impossible to point fingers at anyone, but from my point-of-view, the most likely candidate is Audrey. As my understudy in the play, she's the only one who had a motive, something to gain from my being impaired. And she was with Nikki when the drink was ordered from the bartender. Nikki's also convinced it was Audrey. If so, her efforts were in vain. Rather than let her take over for me, Nigel has decided to put the play on hold while I heal.

"He's no dummy," Nikki says. "He knows the power of publicity. *Day of the Locust* will sell out for sure now."

Of course, the other suspect, I should add, is moi. Given my history, the police think it's more than likely I took the acid of my own volition. And Nikki and Nigel don't rule that out either. Neither does Trey, who's visiting today. He's been coming to see me over the past week between midterms and his job at the country store.

"You really think I dropped acid on purpose?" I ask him.

"I haven't known you for very long so it's hard to say. I don't have a clue how the mind of a drug addict works, just what I've read or seen in movies. I feel bad calling you a drug addict—is there a less harsh term?"

"No. It's accurate. At meetings we introduce ourselves as addicts or alcoholics and there's a reason for that. In order to get better we have to first admit we're powerless over alcohol and drugs."

"It's hard to think of you as being powerless over anything. Your strength and resilience are part of what attracted me to you."

"I don't mean to insult you," I say, "but I need to ask a sensitive question."

"Go for it."

"Did we...?" I pause because I'm trying to find the most appropriate term. There are so many. Trey comes to my rescue.

"No, we did not. You may have short-term memory loss but I don't. We talked about it, though. Do you remember that?"

"I'm sorry, no. What was the conversation?"

"Actually, it was more of a fight."

"We had a *fight?*"

"How do you think you wound up here, all banged up?"

"Stop it," I say, clutching my stomach. "It hurts when I laugh."

Trey pulls his chair closer to the bed. "I kissed you in the back of the country store, and you sort of lashed out at me."

"I did?"

"It got kind of ugly. You said some nasty things. I, on the other hand, was a prince."

"Why would I do that?"

"Something about the fourth step?"

"Ahh. That makes sense. I need to work more of the program before I get into a romantic relationship. Is it okay if we take things slowly?"

Trey lets out a laugh. He takes a photo of me with his phone. "Is there any other way?"

He holds up the photo for me to see. Tubes and bandages and traction and the oh-so-flattering hospital gown. I laugh too.

"Ow! I told you it hurts when I laugh. Don't make me call the nurse. The mean one."

"Sorry, my bad."

Trey gets up and pulls open the drapes to let some light in. It's a clear day and I can see a nice view of L.A. from my bed. He pours himself a Dixie cup of water from my plastic pitcher and downs it.

"There's something I need to talk to *you* about," he says, his tone dead serious. "The night of the accident you said you needed to talk to me about Nikki. Do you remember?"

"No, I don't. Did I say anything else?"

"No, that's it."

"Huh," I say, racking my brain for some clue. It's no use—my memory's shot. "I can't imagine what it might be. Nikki's been a saint through all this. The only time she leaves my side is to take meetings for her upcoming radio show. She's devoted to me, more than my own mom."

"Okay. Maybe it's not important. I just wanted to make sure. I guess I'm having a hard time seeing her career blossom while you take the hits. Maybe I was too benevolent when I rated her on the cray-cray scale. I think she might be a seven. I don't trust her. Something's off. When you're up and around I suggest we do a little sleuthing in that mansion of hers. She's hiding something."

"Now you're scaring me. I agree she's career-driven, but she's taken such good care of me. If I can't trust her, who can I trust?"

"Sorry for scaring you. I'm just sayin'."

A nurse comes in to check my vitals. She picks up a bedpan and asks if I need it.

"I do." I look at Trey. "I think I need to go through all twelve steps before I let you watch this. And even then, I'm not too sure."

"No argument there," he says. He squeezes my hand before he leaves.

• • •

It's been two weeks since the accident. I have crying spells every day, periods of deep depression alternating with bouts of anxiety. I don't understand why anyone would want to harm me. It's frustrating that it's happening at a time when I'm doing everything in my power to be healthy. But all I can do at this point is lie here in bed and trust the doctors know what they're doing.

I'm going home tomorrow, with a cast still on my leg that'll stay there for many weeks to come. I'm limited to bed rest for a while, although soon I'll be able to move around on crutches if I want. A nurse will come by once a week for the first two weeks and once the cast is off I'll begin physical therapy.

Nikki is in the chair next to me, on her laptop. The press is having a field day, and she's checking out the articles. All of them include mention of her and her role as not only my manager, but also sponsor and caregiver.

"The Viper Room is enjoying a resurgence. It hasn't been this popular since River Phoenix kicked the bucket there. People are posting photos on Instagram of the spot where you were hit." She turns her laptop around and shows me the screen.

"For real?" I see a photo of the sidewalk in front of the club. It's filled with gifts from fans—balloons, flowers, teddy bears, and of course, Brianna action figures.

"Is that sweet or perverse?" I ask. "I mean it's not like I died or anything."

"It's sweet *and* perverse, just like Hollywood," Nikki says. "It'd be worse if no one did anything."

"I guess." I look over at the windowsill where another "shrine" to me has been erected. Again, lots of balloons, plants, and flowers. As the nurses brought each one in, they'd read the inscription to me. Aside from a few people from the *Banshee* series, none of the well-wishers are people I know, just fans. It's sad that the people who care about me the most, aside from Nikki and Trey, are perfect strangers. It's Brianna they're seeking to comfort, not me. When I'm better, I want to make a few new friends, healthy friends who I can treat with kindness and respect. Friends I won't lie to, borrow money, or steal from.

Nikki puts her laptop away and soothes my brow with a wet cloth. She gets me a paper cup filled with ice chips and I see that she has tears in her eyes.

"I don't know what I would've done if you had died. I can't take another loss. You mean everything to me, Devon."

I smile at her. "Thank you." I want to express my gratitude more fully but I'm starting to feel the effects of the morphine drip and am having trouble forming thoughts.

"I'm drowsy again. I need to sleep," I say in slurred words. Nikki settles back into her chair, watching over me as I close my eyes. I pray my dreams will offer comfort, not more terror.

# CHAPTER TWELVE

It's good to be back home. As nice as my room was, hospitals are horrible places—all the disinfectants in the world can't seem to cover up the stench of illness and death. And the food sucks too.

I've been here for two weeks and the nurse who comes to change my dressing and check my vitals says I'm healing well, ahead of schedule. Nikki's taking good care of me, cooking meals—or more often, having them delivered from Greenblatt's deli—giving me sponge baths and even dealing with my bedpan, which, thank god, is no longer necessary now that I can get around a bit on crutches.

Nikki's been plugging her new radio show/podcast that's set to start next week. So far she's been on *ET, Extra*, the local news, and *Good Day L.A.* At the moment, I'm watching her *Dr. Phil* appearance that she recorded for me.

"How do you find a needle in a haystack, doc?"

"I don't know, Nikki, how?"

"Lock a junkie in the barn." The audience isn't sure whether to laugh or not. "I've been there and it's true. We addicts are strong-willed. That can be both good and bad."

"So tell me, how is Devon doing?"

"Well, she'll definitely be able to walk again. She was actually very lucky—no head or internal injuries, just some broken bones and bruising. She's staying with me until she recuperates. I call my house the Hokey Pokey clinic—the place to turn yourself around."

Dr. Phil smiles and asks, "And what about her substance abuse? Do you think she'll stay straight?" Phil leans forward and looks terribly concerned.

"Well, they say some folks won't look up until they're flat on their back and that is literally where Devon is at the moment. It's only been a couple of weeks, doc, so it's hard to tell. I'm hoping my cheerleading will convince her she's got what it takes to stay sober. I think she does. But she's living proof that the two hardest things are failure and success and she's experienced both. So have I, although the success part was back in the Jurassic era, I believe." The audience laughs.

"Devon will be fine, Phil, though her ego's taken a big hit. When I was drinking, they used to say, 'Most things can be preserved in alcohol; dignity, however, is not one of them.'"

"Well, Nikki, Devon's certainly lucky to have someone like you to help her through this crisis and work the program. As you said, you've seen some hard times yourself and look at you now." He addresses the audience. "Doesn't she look terrific?" The audience applauds enthusiastically. Nikki gets out of her seat and puts her hands together in prayer. She bows to the studio audience, then once more for the camera.

I flick the TV off.

When I see Nikki on shows like this I can appreciate how she became a star. The woman's got charisma. She comes across as candid and self-deprecating, poking fun at her past exploits as a child-star-gone-bad, which we refer to now simply as CSGB, but also touching when she talks about taking care of me and her crusade against drug abuse.

"I'm going to a morning NA meeting," she says, entering my room. "You got everything you need?"

"Yep, I'm good. Say hi to everyone for me. Maybe I'll be able to join you again in a couple of weeks."

"I hope so. Try and stay in bed. The nurse said you still need lots of rest. Lean forward, sweetie." I do, and she fluffs up my pillow, then smoothes out the blanket and tucks me in. "Ciao."

She leaves and a few moments later I hear the sound of my car driving away. I'm having a hard time dismissing Trey's comment about doing some sleuthing when I'm feeling better. It's killing me that I can't remember what I wanted to talk to him about concerning Nikki. Trey has good instincts so maybe there *is* something about her that's a little crazy, apart from her outward, more obvious eccentricities. With the house to myself, I decide: why wait?

I grab my crutches from the floor and struggle out of bed. My back is sore and my hip is still healing so any movement is still painful. But I'm on a mission and at this point, willing to risk a little pain.

I have to stop twice on my way down the hall to Nikki's bedroom because of the pressure in my hip. Despite the cleaning I did weeks ago it's still a total mess—bed unmade, clothes on the floor, and take-out containers on the nightstand. She always keeps the blinds closed and I wonder if she's a vampire who'd burn up if exposed to light.

I put my crutches aside, sit at her desk, and rummage through the mountains of papers, looking for anything that might raise a red flag. Thankfully, my long-term memory is intact; it's just the events that preceded my accident that have mysteriously vanished like single socks from the dryer.

I find notices for unpaid SAG-AFTRA dues, junk mail, a European postcard from a fan, and five unopened envelopes. They're in a variety of pastel colors with Hallmark embossed on the back. They all have return labels from Pearl Barnes in North Hollywood, which must be Nikki's mom. The postmarks are dated in late April of different years. Birthday cards? I toy with the idea of opening them but decide against it. But they do make me wonder why someone would save unopened cards instead of tossing them. Is there some emotional attachment Nikki still clings to towards her mother—some hope that someday they could repair their relationship?

More rummaging. I find a recent phone bill for Nikki's landline. I look at the numbers she's called but they're meaningless. I'm curious to see if any of them match up with the number Pierce put on my cell the morning he said Nikki had called him. That means staggering back to my room to get my phone—shit! I wrestle with whether or not I'm up to the task and decide I am.

It pays off. Pierce's number is, indeed, one of the phone calls made the morning he was here. So Nikki lied about not knowing him. This triggers a disgusting image in my mind of Nikki going down on Pierce in his black Jaguar. Where did that come from, I wonder? Is it something I actually witnessed that's come back to me as I regain my short-term memory? Or is it just some perverted fantasy?

Feeling terribly pleased with myself, I continue poring over the phone bill. I have another hunch that needs confirming. I've always had an extraordinary ability to remember dates. I'm confident the day of the *Banshee* table read, when I first returned to the studio was the sixteenth. That would make the first on-set rehearsal the seventeenth.

I review all the calls made on the sixteenth and find most of them have 818 or 323 area codes. There's only one that's 310, the area code for Beverly Hills. I call the number on the grimy phone and make a mental note to Purell the hell out of my hands when I'm done. After the second ring I hear a male voice: "Tammy Robbins's office, this is Kevin."

"I'm sorry," I say. "I must have the wrong number." I disconnect. This is exactly what I suspected—Nikki's the one who set up Tammy Robbins's interview with me, pretending to be someone from the staff of *Beverly Hills Banshee*. It's clear now that Nikki's using me to advance her career, or what's left of it. The *People* article put her in the limelight and she's been busy ever since. And I'm sure loving every minute of it. But really, that's no surprise.

As I'm about to hang up the phone, I notice a directory on the inside of the receiver with speed dial names in faded pen. The first is "Mom." I press the button and it rings. A man's gruff voice answers.

"May I speak with Mrs. Barnes, please? Um... *Pearl* Barnes?"

"Who's calling?"

"My name's Devon O'Keefe. I was hoping to speak—"

"She ain't here."

There's a scuffling noise and suddenly I hear a woman's voice that sounds vaguely familiar. "Yes I am!" the woman says. "This is Pearl Barnes. Who is this?"

I concentrate hard and another memory takes shape like a ghost materializing before my eyes. This is the voice I heard several weeks ago informing me she had something important to tell me.

"I live with your daughter. My name's Devon. Did you call me a few weeks ago?"

"Oh, thank god. Yes. Yes, I did. I'm so glad you called back, honey. Listen..."

In the background I hear the man's voice yelling, "Hang up the phone—*now!*"

"Devon, I can't talk now but I've been reading about you and seeing Nikki on the TV programs and..."

"I said hang up the goddamn phone!" the man yells. "Don't make me come over there!"

"You need to get out of that house! Do you understand?" Pearl says.

"No—what are you saying? Is Nikki dangerous?"

"That's enough!" the man yells again. "Don't bring your bitch daughter's trouble into our lives. You got that in your thick skull?"

"Frank, let me talk," Pearl pleads. "Just this once—I promise I won't say too much."

"Please," I say. "Tell me more—can we meet in person?"

I hear more commotion then, "Frank, stop it! Let me finish!" I'm afraid this Frank guy is beating Pearl. Suddenly, the line goes dead.

A dozen thoughts scurry through my mind like roaches when you turn on the light—I'm not sure what to do. If I call back, it might get Pearl in more trouble. Calling the police could have the same result. I take a moment to collect myself then decide there's one more thing I need to do while Nikki's gone.

It's more physically demanding than what I've just endured but I'm up for it. I have to go outside, which means getting down the stairs, something I haven't attempted yet. I use my crutches and travel down the hall to the staircase. I toss them down the stairs so they'll be there when I make it to the bottom, then sit on my ass and slowly slide down, step by painful step, crying, "ouch!" with each bump. At the bottom, I grab the crutches and hoist myself up. The shooting pain in my hips and pelvis is so acute I can barely see straight.

I make my way to the back door, stopping every few feet to let the pain subside. Once outside, I survey the deck and make my way to the open garage. It's dark but I find a bare bulb and pull the string to cast some light on all the junk that's been stored here. I'm looking for any sign of a weapon that might've been used to kill Wheezer. I realize that may sound hysterical, but it's been nagging at me ever since I spoke with Andy. I *think* I spoke with Andy—my memory is patchy.

I start at one end of the garage and systematically search through all the junk as fast as I can, knowing my time is limited. In addition to all the boxes of *One More Thyme* junk we moved in here when I took over the upstairs office, there are shabby suitcases, a rusty old bicycle, Christmas decorations—all of it appearing untouched for decades with crud on everything as it's all been exposed to the weather. I'm overwhelmed and decide to give up my search halfway through as it seems futile—I'm not even sure what I'm looking for. As I head for the back door I spot something gleaming beneath a small shrub outside the garage. I lay my crutches on the ground and crouch down to discover a hatchet. It's just a tool, I tell myself, probably used to hack away at the overgrown prickly pear cacti or jade plants that grow like weeds in Southern California. But I pick it up anyway, fingering the blade that's somewhat dull to the touch. There are tiny traces of what appears to be dried blood on it. Looks like someone cleaned the blood off, possibly by spraying it down with a garden hose but they didn't do a very thorough job. I use my fingernail to pick at the substance and it flakes off. It's definitely dried blood.

As I'm about to set the hatchet down, I notice something even more disturbing—a tiny piece of gray fur stuck on the bloody part of the blade.

It's only a few strands but it's unmistakably Wheezer's—I'd know his fur anywhere. I collapse on the grass feeling nauseated. Someone killed my cat. Probably Nikki. But all I have at this point is circumstantial evidence. How could the person who's taken me in and cared for me so lovingly be capable of such a thing? But the bigger question is *why?*

I recall that first day when I took a photo of Nikki cuddling Wheezer in the driveway. Could that same woman have taken this hatchet and... I can't even think about it.

I pick up a handful of gravel and put it in the pocket of my sweats, then grab my crutches and force myself off the ground, letting out a cry at the stabbing pain in my pelvis. I feel as if my body's just going to break. Like the top half will suddenly snap off from the bottom and my bones and flesh will drop to the ground. My underarms ache, but I'm able to use the crutches to get over to the fence that separates Nikki's property from Andy's. I call out his name but get no response. I reach into my pocket and hurl the small stones at his downstairs windows, then at the second story. Finally, Andy opens his upstairs window yelling, "What the heck are you doing?"

"I need your help!"

• • •

Andy, who I'm discovering is surprisingly strong, is carrying me upstairs to my bedroom. I don't think I could have made the journey myself after all the harm I've just caused to my body. My doctor would plotz if he knew what I've been up to.

Andy places me in bed and sets my crutches down next to it. "Let me make you some hot tea," he says.

"No, I'm worried Nikki will be home soon. I don't want her to find you here."

"Why? You're entitled to have friends."

"I don't want to set her off or cause any sort of suspicion."

"Set her off? What are you talking about?"

"If I'm not careful something bad could happen."

Andy sits down at the end of my bed and looks at me with his sympathetic eyes. "What's going on? Have things with Nikki gotten worse?"

I tell him everything, the facts as well as the suspicions, ending with the bloody hatchet.

"Am I crazy? Do you think Nikki is trying to harm me?"

"You're not crazy. I've known Nikki many years. She's a major whack-job, but so are a lot of people in this canyon; it's one of the things I dig about it. If I wanted normal I'd be living in Encino. But I don't think she's trying to kill you. She could have easily done that by now."

"Then what? Is she just *insane?*"

Andy pulls his hair back, tightens up his pony-tail with the rubber band. He takes a moment to sort his thoughts. When he speaks, his tone reminds me of the many therapists I've seen through the years—measured and calm.

"There's a pattern to Nikki's behavior. She creates trauma for you, then comes to your rescue. I'm reminded of something that happened a few years ago. I treated a girl. Imogen. Probably about eleven or twelve. She had chronic vomiting, dehydration, and abdominal pain. I'll never forget her long, woebegone face, and how painfully thin she was. Her mother had taken her to a bunch of specialists and none could find the source of her symptoms. That's why her mother brought her to me—to explore non-traditional therapies. I saw her for about six months and tried every form of healing I know, but nothing helped. Imogen died. They did an autopsy but couldn't determine the cause of her death." Andy's voice becomes shaky—clearly the loss of this girl is still an open wound for him.

"I'm so sorry," I say.

"Several months later," he continues, "the mother returned with her eight-year-old son, Jeremiah. Same thing. He had all the symptoms his sister had but the doctors couldn't find a damn thing wrong with him. This young boy had dark circles under his eyes and never smiled. About a year later he died too."

"Did they do an autopsy on *him?*" I ask.

"Yeah, turned up zip. So they did further investigating. A toxicology analysis of the boy's tissues revealed dramatically elevated arsenic levels.

So they did an analysis of tissues saved from the sister and found they had a high liver arsenic level too."

"The mother was poisoning her kids?"

Andy nods. "So she could devote herself to 'taking care' of them."

"I don't get it."

"The craving for attention. And sympathy. It's a mental illness, Munchausen-by-Proxy syndrome. I did some research. It's named after the fictional Baron Munchausen who was based on an eighteenth century German dignitary famous for making up shit about his travels and experiences in order to get attention. Because the parent or caregiver appears to be so sympathetic and attentive, as you've described Nikki, no one suspects any foul play."

"You think Nikki's been feeding my addiction so she can keep rescuing me?"

"I don't know. She certainly fits the profile—needy, unstable, craves attention."

"It's true. I've never met anyone as nurturing as Nikki. And she *has* been getting lots of attention since caring for me. Not just from doctors and nurses but because we're celebrities, from people we don't even know."

Andy stands. "Let me move you out of here. Right now—before she comes home. You can stay at my house—I have plenty of room."

This, of course, makes perfect sense. And if I were watching someone in my situation in a movie, I'd be yelling at the screen, "Get the hell out of there!" and be irritated if they didn't. But my instincts are telling me to stay. Nikki's due home any minute and I'd be putting Andy in danger. If she butchered my cat, there's no telling what she's capable of. I couldn't live with myself if I caused this kind man harm.

I also feel the need to take control of my life. I'm sick of being a damsel in distress; it's time to go *mano a mano* with Nikki, whatever that might entail. She's my problem, not anyone else's. I'm the one who ignored all the red flags, but that's over now. It's up to me to plan my escape. Of course I can't tell Andy this—he just wants me out of here.

"There's not enough time," I say. Nikki'll be home any minute."

"So? If she went off on us, you don't think I could kick her bony ass? I'm a black belt, you know. I'm not afraid of her. I'll tell her I'm moving you out."

"No, we have to *plan* an escape. Plus, I think I really injured myself today. I don't think it's a good idea for me to be moved that far. I ache all over."

"I'm worried about you, Devon. Remember I told you to trust your instincts? You're not doing that."

"Yes, I am," I say, and mean it.

"Look me in the eyes and tell me you're not frightened."

"Of course I am. But I'm safe at the moment. Nikki's told half the world I'm bedridden and that she's taking care of me."

"Then let me call 911."

"Oh, God no! No more publicity!"

Andy realizes he's getting nowhere with me. "You're more concerned with publicity than getting yourself killed?"

"Geez, when you phrase it like that..."

"You're not thinking rationally. You're in a state of trauma." He gently pats my good leg. "Trust me on this one."

"Okay, maybe you're right about the trauma. But people respect you. I'm a bad joke. Every time I make the news, a part of me dies."

Andy sighs. "So what's your plan?"

"Give me your phone number. I promise I'll call as soon as Nikki leaves the house again. That'll give us enough time to get me and my things over to your house."

Andy sighs again, then tells me his cell number which I punch into my phone. He gets up and heads for the door.

"All right," he says, "I can't drag you away against your will. I'm going now," and I can hear the weariness in his voice. He turns and points at me. "I'll be waiting for your call."

"Thanks, Andy. Now please leave before Nikki comes back."

"Namaste," he says, turning those three syllables into a prayer for me.

"Namaste," I repeat.

# CHAPTER THIRTEEN

Moments after Andy leaves, I hear the car pull up. I quickly turn on the TV and pretend I'm watching it. In a blast of irony, the show that comes on is a rerun of *Growing Pains*, starring the trifecta of CSGB, Gary Coleman, Dana Plato, and Todd Bridges. Why is it so many child stars grow up to live such sad lives as adults? What is it about fame that destroys people? No time to ponder that—Nikki enters my room, talking a mile a minute.

"Everyone sends their love. I told them how quickly you're healing and how you'll be up and walking again in a few weeks, if all goes well. And I plugged my new radio show and..." Suddenly she stops talking and cocks her head like a dog. She sniffs the air.

"Do you smell that?"

"No, what?" I ask.

"Incense."

"Huh," I say. "It's probably my hand lotion. I just—"

"No. It's incense." She looks me right in the eye. "Sandalwood."

I hold her gaze, neither of us looking away. The sound of abrasive canned laughter from the TV fills the room.

"Was Andy here?" Nikki asks.

"Andy? No. No, he wasn't here." I'm a terrible liar.

"It's okay if he was, I'm just asking."

"Well, he wasn't. I wouldn't lie to you."

She's not buying it. "You know, if it weren't for me you'd be living in some shithole in Reseda, smoking crack."

"Whoa—where did *that* come from?"

"I think you know," she says, then turns around and leaves the room. "Definitely sandalwood," she says under her breath.

· · ·

I nap, and when I awaken, I'm in severe pain. And I need to pee. When Nikki enters with my lunch tray I ask for the bedpan.

"Really? You didn't need it this morning. In fact, you said you were feeling a whole lot better. How come you need it now?"

"I can't use the crutches anymore. I'm in a lot of pain."

"And why do you think that is?" she says smugly as she sets the tray down on the nightstand and sits on the end of my bed.

"Um... I don't know. I think I might've done something while I was taking a nap. I toss and turn a lot."

"Then let's go to the hospital."

I consider this, but can't trust that Nikki will actually take me there, especially now that she suspects I'm on to her. It's safer to stick with Plan Andy.

"No, no, I'm not in that much pain."

"You just said you're in a lot of pain. Which is it? The nurse who was here *twice* said you were healing nicely. Ahead of schedule she said. What the hell's going on with you?"

"What do you *mean?*"

"Devon, I know you were walking around today. I could see the imprints of your crutches in the dirt near the garage."

Hmm, she doesn't mention anything about the hatchet, which I now realize I stupidly didn't put back under the shrub.

"Guilty as charged. Yes, I was walking around and it was totally dumb of me. I thought some fresh air and exercise might do me good. Guess I was wrong."

"And P.S.," she adds, "I know you were in my bedroom. It may look messy, but trust me—there's a method to my madness. I know where every piece of paper belongs."

"Your papers? What would I want with them?"

"You tell me. Or maybe it was your Chinese friend, Mr. Chiu who was after something."

"Nikki!"

"I know he was here—I can smell that incense shit a mile away."

"What does his being Chinese have to do with anything? Why would you even *mention* that?"

"Don't change the subject! Admit it—he was here!"

"Okay, Andy was here. He was visiting me—what's wrong with that?"

"Apparently something, otherwise you wouldn't have lied to me." Good point. She challenges me with a 'what do you have to say about that?' look.

"I know this sounds silly," I say, "but I thought you might be jealous. You tend to be possessive with me and I didn't want to set you off."

"Ooh, I like that—'*set me off*'—like I'm some sort of batshit wacko who flies off the handle."

"I don't want to argue with you, Nikki, I just want the bedpan."

She goes into the bathroom and comes back with it. As I'm using it, she starts to stroke my hair. I pull away.

"Can I just pee alone, please, without your hands all over me?"

"Look, Devon," Nikki says as she takes the pan from me and heads into the bathroom, "I told you I'm doing the best I can and hopefully you'll come to understand that. Nobody's willing to take care of you the way I am." She enters the room with the clean bedpan, which she places next to my bed. "Certainly not Andy Chiu."

She looks directly at me. Her lips are trembling. "That man's experimented with more drugs than you and I put together. Peyote. Shrooms. Ayahuasca. He's the last person in the world you want overseeing your health care. He's a wasted old hippie and you'd be wise to stay away from him."

"Okay. I will."

Her demeanor changes in a flash.

"Gotta go," she says cheerfully. "I have to prepare for my radio show; it starts tomorrow."

"You're leaving?"

"Yep."

I can't believe my good fortune. If all goes well, I'll have my life back in a matter of hours.

"See you later, sweetie," Nikki says in a voice dripping with honey, then leaves the room.

I wait for the sound of her footsteps bounding down the stairs, then reach for my purse on the floor. I rummage around in it but no phone. The outlet near my bed is bare; the charger is gone too. Nikki must've taken both while I was napping. If that weren't bad enough, I see my laptop is no longer on the dresser. I'm totally cut off from the world and in intense pain.

"Nikki!" I scream, which only makes the pain worse. I hear the sound of her opening then closing the front door. So much for trusting my instincts and taking matters into my own hands. This is exactly what I deserve.

I'm so angry at myself I sweep the lunch tray onto the floor. Food flies everywhere: peanut butter and jelly on a piece of stale white bread and a few potato chips. The quality of my meals has declined noticeably—no more Greenblatt's deli, now it's just whatever Nikki happens to have on hand. Just as well, I think. It's probably poisoned.

I need to get out of here now. I can see Andy's Jacuzzi from my bed, but he's not in it, just his cat sleeping peacefully on one of the benches. I carefully ease myself onto the floor and shove one of my crutches ahead of me. Using my arms and upper body strength, I scooch my way over to the window, then jam the rubber crutch bottom against the top of the wood frame to open it. I call out Andy's name a few times but get no response, so I struggle back to bed, crying because the shooting pain in my hips, pelvis, and legs is unbearable. I've really done serious damage to myself when I ventured downstairs. What I need, other than a good doctor, is complete bed rest. But that's not possible anymore. If I want to survive, I have to move.

My next thought is to get to the landline in Nikki's bedroom and call 911. The police will be able to break down the front door to get to me.

I decide to try a new approach to movement: rolling. I lie down on my side, my body fully stretched out, and roll myself as slowly as possible toward the door. It hurts a lot but not as much as the other methods I've tried and if I go slowly enough, I think I can make it. It takes about twenty minutes to reach the door and getting through it is another challenge entirely. I'm forced to curl into a fetal position, then roll, which is much more painful than the straight rolling. I cry out in agony, but make it through. Then it's another fifteen minutes of slowly rolling down the hallway to Nikki's room and through the door in the painful fetal position again.

I reach up to her desk and grab the phone. I lift the receiver and bring it to my ear. No dial tone. The line is dead. Of course it is.

I fight back the urge to weep because I no longer have that luxury; it would only make the pain worse. They say the Alaskan Natives have fifty or a hundred words for snow. I wonder why we don't have more words for pain because my body is riddled with every kind imaginable. In addition to the stabbing pain in my legs and pelvis and the flu-like achiness in every other part of my body, I now feel a pressure in my head, behind my eyes. There's no way I can make it downstairs and to the front door. I reach into the pocket of my sweat pants where I keep my painkillers. I'm not so dumb that I leave them where Nikki can get her hands on them. It's been over six hours since my last dose, so I pop a Percocet and swallow it without water. Closing my eyes, I take a deep breath, then begin the agonizing journey back to bed.

• • •

It's 9:07 PM when I awake. No sign of Nikki but the food I trashed has been cleaned up. There's no dinner tray, which is too bad since I'm shaky and need to eat.

I realize this is the time Andy usually meditates in his Jacuzzi. I look out the window and see him in the bubbling water, his eyes closed. As usual, his CD player sits on one of the wooden benches on the deck, playing ancient Chinese music. His cat, Chimon, sleeps on the other bench. It's foggy and a dreamlike white mist blankets the night.

Suddenly, his cat becomes alert, rising up on his haunches. A robed, barefooted figure emerges from the mist: it's Nikki. She's on Andy's side of the fence, quietly crossing the lawn. She steps onto Andy's deck, behind him. Oh God, she's going to confront him about meddling into her "caregiving." This is good—Andy won't stand for it; he'll use force if he needs to.

As Nikki heads toward the benches, Chimon looks at her, arches his back and hisses. I let out a dry laugh. Even this animal can sense Nikki's evil presence. Nikki takes a few more steps toward the bench and I assume she's going to turn off the CD player so she can confront Andy. Then a darker thought strikes and the horror of what's about to happen registers.

I need to warn Andy and there's no time to do that delicately. I throw myself on the floor, grab my crutch and pound on the window with it.

"Andy! Get out of there! Now!" His eyes remain closed, the churning waters of the Jacuzzi drowning me out.

Nikki reaches for the CD player that's plugged into a socket under the bench via a long extension cord. I rip off the rubber tip of my crutch, banging hard on the window with the metal end. The glass shatters. I use my elbow to clear away the shards of glass and stick my head out the window.

"Andy! Andy, get out of there!" He opens his eyes and looks up at me.

"Quick! Get out of the water! Now!" He looks confused, doesn't see Nikki until I point to her. "Look! Jesus Christ, Andy, get out of there!" I'm sobbing now. Nikki's at the Jacuzzi's edge holding the CD player.

"Nikki, don't! Please, don't do it!" Andy sees her and starts to get up. But not before Nikki throws the player into the water.

I scream as Andy is electrocuted, his body twitching and gyrating uncontrollably like a possessed marionette. Chimon freaks out, letting loose a screech that blends with the sound of the hissing water. I watch in shock as Nikki tip-toes across the grass to the garden hose. She turns it on and sprays down the deck, washing away all traces of her wet footprints. As she climbs over the low fence, I crumple to the floor, bawling uncontrollably. "Oh my God! Oh my God!" I pound the floor, then my chest, my gut. My stomach contracts violently and vomit erupts from my coughing, choking mouth. I wipe it with my sleeve, then retch again and once more, bringing up a clear, acidic liquid that burns my throat. I destroy the room, my prison. Crutches tossed, furniture hurled, pictures knocked off walls. I throw myself on the bed, my body in a blinding pain that doesn't begin to deliver the suffering I deserve.

# CHAPTER FOURTEEN

I awake in the late morning to the sound of hammering and the din of a
too-loud TV set. Nikki's boarding up my window with lumber. I look
around, see the destruction of my room. My brain is foggy, but it starts
to piece together the events of last night. I close my eyes and am jolted by
an image so shocking I assume it must be the remnants of a bad dream.
But somehow I know it's real.

Nikki stops hammering when she sees something on the TV. "Oh,
there it is," she says. "The local news." A male reporter stands in front of
Andy Chiu's house. People are placing wreaths, candles and flowers on a
makeshift shrine at his doorstep.

"This quiet Laurel Canyon neighborhood in the Hollywood Hills is
mourning the loss of one of its most beloved residents, sixty-six year-old
Andy Chiu," the reporter says. "Chiu died a violent death by electrocu-
tion last night when his pet cat knocked a CD player into his Jacuzzi.
A much-celebrated healer, Chiu practiced alternative Eastern medicine
and treated many celebrities including Corey Feldman, Linda Blair, and
Britney Spears."

The camera pans to the right and I see Nikki standing next to the
reporter. The reporter continues: "I'm standing here with Andy Chiu's

next-door neighbor and close friend, actress Nikki Barnes. Nikki, tell us what you saw last night."

"I was outside on my deck, talking on the phone. It was about nine o' clock, I think. And I heard this kind of loud splash, you know, coming from next door. Then I heard a scream and the sound of hissing water, kind of like steam. I looked over and saw Andy's cat running away from the Jacuzzi. I climbed over our fence and that's when I saw..." Nikki pauses for effect, as if she's too traumatized to speak. "...my dear friend and neighbor, Andy Chiu. His body was lifeless in the water." She wipes tears from her eyes. Real tears, not those created with a menthol tear stick that some actors use. I think I've underestimated Nikki's acting abilities. "His CD player was just floating there, with smoke rising from it. It was still plugged in." She cries again as if she's overcome with grief. "Sorry, guys, I can't do this," she says as she leaves the frame.

"Thank you," says the reporter whose talking head now fills the screen. "Police say there will be a full investigation into the death. A memorial service will be held on..." Nikki flicks off the TV.

"So sad," she says as if she's just watched a tear-jerking chick-flick. She has no more interest in the story—her performance is over. She goes back to the window and finishes hammering the last board, saying, "Just in time. There's supposed to be a series of storms heading our way. El Niño." She comes over and sits on my bed.

"I'm sorry about your friend," she says gently. "Sometimes it helps to have a good cry, get it all out of your system."

"You're *sorry?* What are you *talking* about? You *killed* him!"

"What? Don't be ridiculous. His cat caused the accident. You saw it on the news, same as I did. You know, you got quite a dose of LSD in your system. It causes flashbacks and hallucinations. I think you're confusing them with reality."

I'm incapable of a response. No words could make sense of this.

Nikki gets up and brings me water. "Drink up," she says, feeding it to me through a bendable straw. I drink the whole glass—my body's a sponge.

"Water's great, Nikki, but I also need food. I haven't eaten since yesterday morning. That's three meals you've kept from me, four if you don't bring me lunch before you go."

"Actually, I read that the human body can go three weeks without food. Ask Gandhi."

"I will," I say. "I'll probably be seeing him real soon."

Nikki laughs. "Don't be such a drama queen," she says, taking away the empty glass.

"I need a doctor, Nikki. I need to go to the hospital."

No response.

"I won't say a word to anyone. I promise."

Again, nothing. Nikki leaves and returns a moment later with an old radio she sets on top of my nightstand.

"I'm doing my first show today. It's live at 1:00. Be sure to listen—I'll be talking about you."

"What will you say? That I'm dying a slow death, trapped in a room without any way of communicating to the outside world? That I'm grieving for the innocent man you killed? Or will you lie like you always do?"

"Chill, Devon. No one's dying a slow death. She plugs the radio into the socket. "And Andy's cat killed him—it was an accident. We've been through this already. Don't play games with me."

"I'm not playing games. And I'm not crazy. I know what I saw."

"I don't understand where this anger is coming from. I'm doing my best to take care of you. Moving you downstairs and into a car would be the worst thing for your body."

"Then call a fucking ambulance!" I scream.

"An *ambulance?* Do you know how many paparazzi are out there right now? Is that really what you want?"

"I want to live, Nikki. That's what I want."

"Then you have to regain my trust. No more stunts like dropping acid at the Viper. I can't take any chances that you'll somehow get your hands on more drugs, prescription or otherwise. All I can do is keep you safe here in this room until you're better. I wish you could understand that."

She looks down at me, waiting for a response.

"Oh, I understand, Nikki. You're sick. You need help."

Nikki lets out a bitter laugh. "Oh, now *I'm* the sick one?"

"I think you know what I mean." She turns her back on me, heads for the door.

"You're worse than my mother. You don't know what the fuck you're talking about."

"I do. Please. You have an illness—you need to see someone about it."

Nikki pivots around to face me. Her expression is one I haven't seen before and it scares me. Her face is pinched and tense, like a feral animal. Her voice changes too as she raises the volume, becoming coarse and guttural. It's as if I've awakened a sleeping beast.

"You're an ingrate, you know that?" She pulls a cigarette out of the pocket of the oversized, men's shirt she's wearing. She lights it, takes a drag, then lets out a stream of smoke that makes me cough. With the window boarded up, there's no fresh air in the room. What I wouldn't give to be outside hiking with Trey.

"I've provided you with nothing but kindness," Nikki continues, nervously pacing the room as she smokes. "I took you in off the street, put a roof over your head, gave you a bed to sleep in. I've treated you like my own daughter—fed you, bathed you, cleaned up your vomit, emptied your shit-filled bedpan."

I'm beginning to think she believes her own lies. Jesus—that would make her psychotic. I try a different tack. "I'm sorry. I really do appreciate everything you've done for me. All I'm saying is, I need medical attention."

Nikki sits at the end of my bed and takes a drag on her cigarette. I wonder if anything I've said has broken through to her.

"We can talk about it when I get back."

"Okay, but before you go, can I please have some lunch?"

"So you can throw it on the floor again? I don't think so. You need to learn there are consequences to your actions. It's in the program. When you behave, I'll bring you food."

"And my cell—when can I have it back? I need to call my mom. She's probably worried about me."

Nikki looks at me like I'm nuts.

"You can stay in the room while I call," I say. "I just want to hear her voice."

"Your mom? The woman who came all the way from Minnesota or wherever the hell you're from and couldn't get on that return flight fast enough? Is that who we're talking about?"

"Yes."

"Or is it really Trey's voice you want to hear?"

I stop breathing for a moment. I haven't heard from Trey in two days. Did she off him too?

"Did he call for me?" I ask. "Did you talk to him?"

"Of course I did. He wanted to come visit, but we can't have that right now." She speaks more calmly now, the voice of reason. "God knows what bacteria he's exposed to working in that scummy country store. You're susceptible to getting an infection—we can't risk visitors."

Nikki gets up to smooth out the bedspread. "Lean forward," she says. I do and she fluffs up my pillow. I lay my head back down. She sits on the bed near me and strokes my hair with one hand while bringing the other to her mouth for one last puff of her cigarette. I want to recoil but don't.

"So... Trey. He wanted to see me? What exactly did you tell him?"

"There's not much to say," she says, dropping the cigarette butt on the carpet and putting it out with her sneakered foot. "I told him *and* your friends at the theatre that you're at your mom's for a few weeks, recuperating. He's been calling and texting like crazy; he's really turning into a pest."

*Oh, Christ, I'm going to die in this room.*

"Besides," Nikki continues. "You don't want a player like Trey. My God, he's fucked every chick in the canyon."

She looks at me, but I don't give her the satisfaction of a response. What she says could be true, I guess. I don't really know Trey that well, but he just doesn't seem like the type that indiscriminately hooks up.

Nikki stands. "I realize my methods may piss you off sometimes, but try and remember I just want you to get well. Because I love you."

"You don't know anything about love."

"Think what you like, Devon, but just remember, your fate is in my hands. *I'm* your higher power now." She flashes a smile and leaves the room. I pull out my last Percocet and pop it into my mouth. I'm hoping it'll knock me out so I won't be tempted to turn on Nikki's radio show. I've suffered enough already.

• • •

Nikki comes in every so often to give me water but food is scarce—a spoonful of yogurt, a piece of cheese, sometimes a slice of turkey if I'm lucky. Just enough to keep me alive.

• • •

Nikki's visits are filled with chatter. She blathers on about everything, all in her most pleasant voice as if everything is peachy-keen. "Devon," she'll say, with a laugh in her voice, "at my meeting today, a big fat cow of a man comes in and sits on a folding chair. The suspense was unbearable—is it going to collapse? Is he going to fall off? After someone gets up to share, he realizes he's in the wrong place—he meant to go to an OA meeting instead! 'I thought everyone looked a little thin,' he says and suddenly the room was up for grabs."

Or she'll tell me about her radio program. "My producer is a total asshole," she'll say. "He gets all flustered when I talk about sex on the air even though sexual addiction is part of my gig. 'Um, Nikki,' he says. 'Do you think you could tone it down a bit?' I egg him on: 'What are you talking about?' 'You know, the graphic stuff,' he says. 'Graphic? Can you be more specific?' He tries to tell me, but he keeps stuttering and I don't know what the fuck he's trying to say. I love to make him blush, so I help him out: 'You mean jacking off? Or double-penetration? Stuff like that?' 'Yeah, stuff like that,' he says, making a beeline for the door. And he's off, quicker than a prom dress!"

I don't respond. I've stopped speaking to her. What's the point?

• • •

I'm pretty sure it's early afternoon, so I lean over and turn on the radio. After a few commercials and the news I hear, *ReKovery with Nikki* for the first time. Her theme song is, I'm not kidding, "I Will Survive," Gloria Gaynor's disco anthem. *Really?* She couldn't find anything a little less obvious?

Nikki greets her listeners, makes a few jokes about recovery, then announces, "It's time to welcome today's guest, Jeannette Bailey, another child-star-gone-bad. Most of you know Jeannette from the classic sitcom, *Kissin' Kuzzins*, one of my favorites."

"Thank you, sweet cakes," she says to Nikki in a heavy southern accent. "I'm just so tickled to be here today, chatting with you after so many years."

*Kissin' Kuzzins* was on about twenty-five years ago, long before my time, but I've seen plenty of reruns in syndication. Jeannette started out when she was an adorable eight-year-old. She went through the typical awkward stage most adolescents suffer and it was at that time she was written off the series—her character suddenly became an exchange student overseas. A younger, more adorable character replaced her, making the network executives happy. After that, Jeanette had trouble getting any kind of role and eventually settled for voiceover work for kids cartoons. For a while, there was a sex tape floating around on the Internet, but Jeannette swore it wasn't her. Who knows? After that, she started selling a line of gaudy jewelry on the Home Shopping Network and she hasn't acted since.

"Like me, Jeannette, you've overcome your share of hardships and are now clean and sober. So tell me and our listeners—how did you turn your life around?"

"Well, it wasn't me, Nikki. The credit for that goes to the Lord."

There's a noticeable pause and I'm picturing Nikki smiling through gritted teeth and wondering how to proceed. She believes in the concept of a higher power, but she's not the least bit religious, in fact, she told me she became an atheist after Julia died.

"Uh-huh," Nikki finally says. "I assume you're referring to a 'higher power,' which can be just about anythin—"

"I'm referring to Jesus Christ, my personal savior. He spilled his blood for me."

"His blood."

"Yes, ma'am. He works in strange ways, that one. A year ago I was turning tricks in an alley and today I'm the proud mama of a precious baby girl."

"So you're a new mother?" Nikki says, grateful they've moved on from Jesus. "Congratulations!"

"Thank you. And just as the Lord saved me," she says, starting to tear up, "he's sure enough going to watch over Cheyenne, my little crack-addicted angel. I just know he is."

I can't believe what I'm listening to. *This* is how Nikki wants to affect positive change for troubled teens?

"The point is, listeners," she says, tying to get back on track, "no matter how lost you are, there's always a way back."

"Praise the Lord."

"But addicts don't often ask for help, do they, Jeannette?"

"No, ma'am, they sure don't."

"We have to recognize the signs of trouble and help our loved ones, whether they want it or not. As listeners of my show know, all my energy these days goes into the rehabilitation of my dear friend, Devon O'Keefe, the former star of *Beverly Hills Banshee*. Devon was hit by a car recently while tripping on acid. The good news is her body is pretty much healed, and she's totally drug-free. The unfortunate news is that, as is often the case with addicts, she's replaced one disorder with another."

*Wait—what?*

"I'm sorry to report we're currently waging a war against anorexia nervosa. I have the best eating disorder experts in the country caring for her around the clock. But your cards and letters, texts and tweets—"

"And prayers," Jeannette pipes in.

"—will be greatly appreciated."

"If you want to be updated on Devon's progress you can follow me on Twitter or—"

I turn off the radio, resisting the impulse to throw it against the wall. I know now that everything Andy suspected is true. Nikki's going to bring me to the brink of starvation, publicize the hell out of it, then nurse me back to health and reap all the attention she craves so much. I wonder if on some subconscious level she really believes she's doing good, that her illness prevents her from acknowledging how destructive she is.

She doesn't seem worried that I'm going to tell the world what she's up to. Probably because I have zero credibility—anything I say is questionable—the rantings of someone who's ingested far too many drugs.

Or maybe she's planning on actually letting me starve to death, then getting attention in the form of sympathy. "I tried my best," I can hear her say, "but anorexia is a powerful disease." Every thought I have ultimately leads back to the grim reality that I'm probably going to die in this horrible house ruled by the punked-out evil queen of Laurel Canyon. My only hope is that Trey or someone from the theatre will hear her crappy radio show and figure out I'm still in L.A. and not recovering in Wisconsin. Nikki didn't think that one through. I guess that's typical of pathological narcissists—they believe they're impervious to just about everything.

I try to sleep, but taking the Percocet on an empty stomach has made me nauseated. I'm afraid I might barf in my sleep and choke on my own vomit. I guess there are worse ways to die. Being stomped to death like the little kid at the end of *Day of the Locust*. Or being electrocuted in a Jacuzzi.

I can't think straight. Did Nikki really kill Andy? Or could the image I can't get out of my head actually be a hallucination from the acid? I don't know anything anymore. I hurt all over. My bones. My head. I'm hungry and thirsty—the water pitcher Nikki usually keeps filled is empty. I miss Wheezer.

# *PEARL*

# CHAPTER FIFTEEN

Nina, the gal next door, stops by to check on me. Pretty young thing, must be about twenty, I 'spose. Lives with her boyfriend. He's got a good job, works at a pest control company.

"Oh, Pearl," she says, sighing. "What am I going to do with you? Frank hit you again, didn't he?"

There's no use lying to her. I've got a shiner the size of I don't know what. "He only hits me when he drinks," I say. What I don't say is the bastard drinks all day, every day.

"Why won't you let me help you? I did some research." She pulls a piece of paper out of her pocket, hands it to me. "There's a women's shelter not too far from here in Van Nuys. For abused wives."

"I'm not an abused wife. And Frank's not my husband." I push the paper back to her, across the kitchen table.

"Stop it, Pearl," she says. "You know what I mean." She takes the paper, puts it in my hand. I stick it in the pocket of my housecoat. No use fighting with her.

"A couple more days and I'll be able to go out again without sunglasses."

"That's not the point. You don't need to put up with this. You deserve better."

"What if I was to tell you I don't deserve better? That I deserve some-one like Frank. Someone who treats me like crap."

"I'd say you just need some counseling. I can get you the name of someone who could help you. They work on a sliding fee scale so you wouldn't have to pay much."

I can't see myself doing that—going to a fancy psychiatrist. I look down at the table wishing this conversation would end.

"What have you done that makes you think you deserve this?" Nina asks.

"Nothing. Forget I ever said anything. I'm okay, Nina. Thanks for stopping by. You want some coffee cake to take with you? I've got some nice coffee cake."

Nina gets up. "No thanks, Pearl. But if you change your mind about getting help, you let me know. And if you need anything, Spencer and I are right next door." She starts to leave my apartment, then stops in her tracks and turns around.

"Oh, I almost forgot. Your daughter's got a new radio show. Have you heard it?"

"No. What do you mean, radio show? She plays music?"

"No, it's a talk show. It's on every weekday at 1:00. She has guests, and people call in. It's about drug abuse—you know, she gives advice and stuff to teenagers."

"Oh, lord."

• • •

At first I think I don't want to hear anything Nicole has to say. But I can't help it. I'm curious. So I turn on her talk show while Frank's passed out on the couch after another bender. Nicole's yappin' to some teenag-er who's a crystal meth addict. She tries to get her to go to a Narcotics Anonymous meeting. "Where do you live, sweetie?" Nicole asks the girl.

"In the valley," the girl says. "Canoga Park."

"I'll come by and personally take you to a meeting," Nicole says. "Hang on the line after our call and my assistant will set it up." Oh, please. Nicole's a saint. A goddamn saint. After the commercial, she starts running her mouth about anorexia. She's trying to sound like a medical expert or something, but I can tell she's reading something someone else wrote.

"Between five to twenty percent of individuals struggling with anorexia nervosa will die," she says. "Anorexia has one of the highest death rates of any mental health condition. It's the most common cause of death—up to twelve times higher than any other condition among young women ages fifteen to twenty-four."

I remember when Nicole was on her television show years ago. Some big-shot producer pulled me aside and says, "Your daughter needs to lose some weight. Fifteen pounds," he says. I didn't think she looked heavy, but I didn't want her to lose her job so I talked to her about it. We didn't know about things like this anorexia back then. Or what is it, bulimia. So I didn't do anything when Nicole lost the weight. I could hear her throwing up in the bathroom after meals, but like I said, I didn't want her to lose her job. Now I know better.

Nicole's still going on about anorexia. Not sure why—I thought her program was 'sposed to be about drugs and the like. Then she says something about Devon O'Keefe and I get it. Nicole's telling her listeners that Devon's stayed sober, but she's lost a lot of weight in the past couple a weeks. Nicole's worried about her.

"Please continue to send your cards, texts, and tweets to the show and I'll make sure Devon gets them," she says, pretending to cry. She's quite an actress, better than everyone thinks. "They may help. But as we all know, there's only so much we can do in cases like this. Devon's the only one who can make herself better, and she's not there yet. She's literally starving herself. I know what she's going through because I've been there myself when I was her age. It's a self-esteem issue and Devon's ego has certainly suffered over the past few months, not just because of her much-publicized bouts with drugs, but also getting fired from her TV series."

Then Nicole starts up with all she's doing for Devon and I get this bad feeling in my stomach.

"I've brought in the best experts in the field and they've all tried to convince Devon to enter a treatment facility, but she refuses. Her body mass index just dipped below fifteen so things are pretty extreme. But she's an adult and you can't commit someone against their will, unfortunately."

Frank's passed out cold and I got just enough time to get to Nicole's place and back if I take his car. But I haven't driven in years and it's storming real bad what with the El Niño business and all. I figure it should take me about fifteen minutes to get from North Hollywood to Laurel Canyon. Nicole's been on the air for only about ten minutes so I've got some time. I put on my raincoat, grab my umbrella and pocketbook, and step out into the storm.

Rain always reminds me of a joke me and Nicole used to share. "I hope this keeps up," she'd say. "Why?" I'd ask even though I already knew the answer. "So it doesn't come down!" she'd say. Corny joke, but I'd always make sure to laugh like it was the funniest thing I ever heard. Sometimes I miss that Nicole, the cute little girl who didn't have a care in the world. Don't know why I pushed her into show business—seemed like a good idea at the time.

• • •

The weather's bad enough in the valley, but when I climb into the hills the winds pick up something fierce. There's a downed cell phone tower on Laurel Canyon Boulevard near that country store and a few fellas are working to repair it. It's been years since I drove these roads to Nicole's house, but I remember the way as if it was yesterday. Brings back bad memories, lots of bad memories.

I get to Nicole's house and park along the curb where water is rushing downhill. I put on the emergency brake so the car's not swept away by a flash flood. I open my umbrella, but a second later it gets turned inside out by the strong winds. I throw the useless piece of crap in the gutter.

Nicole's house gives me the willies. Looks pretty much the same as I remembered, only more shabbier. The trim is chipped and peeling like it hasn't been painted in thirty years. The bougainvillea's taken over. I'm not surprised—it grows like a weed even if you don't take care of it at all. There's a flash of lightning and the whole house lights up for a split second, just like in one of those old horror pictures with Vincent Price or whoever. And that's just what this old falling apart mansion is to me, a house of horrors.

I ring the doorbell but no one answers. I press it again, over and over, but still no one comes. I try and remember where Nicole left a spare key. I pick up a few potted cactuses on the stoop and sure enough I find the key under one of them. I open the door and go inside.

It's dark. Not a light on in the whole darn house. I turn on a lamp and look around. The place looks just like I remembered it, only worse. I raised Nicole right, and always kept a clean house myself, but this is a pigsty.

"Hello?" I call out. "Devon! It's Pearl Barnes—Nicole's, I mean... Nikki's mom! You here, honey?" No one answers, so I walk around the living room and into the den. The place is empty, so I go upstairs.

"Don't be scared, dear!" I yell. "It's Pearl. I'm here to help you!"

I grip the iron banister as I climb the staircase, but I get winded and have to stop every few steps. I walk down the dark hallway to check out each room, not sure where the girl might be. I wonder if she's even here at all.

I peek into the first room, the master bedroom, I think. I turn on the overhead light, but there's no sign of Devon, just a lot of Nicole's mess. I open the next door I come to and before I even so much as turn on the light I know it's Julia's room—it smells just like I remember, only musty. I turn on a lamp and see a whole bunch of dolls lining the room, all different kinds—on the bed, the dresser, the toy chest. Every time Julia had to stay in the hospital, Nicole bought her a new one. Next to a couple of Barbies is a Jennifer Thyme doll, skinny as a twig. She looks so much like Nicole at that age it gives me the heebie-jeebies. I turn off the light real quick and shut the door.

I keep going down the hallway to the last room, Nicole's office. There's a padlock on the door. Holy crap. "You in there, honey?"

I put my ear to the door but don't hear anything.

"Devon?" I call out again and then I knock hard on the door—nothing. I put my ear to the door again and this time I hear something. Not words, just a low sort of whimper, like the sound of a small animal in pain. Oh, Christ.

"Don't worry, honey," I shout. "I'm going to get you out of there." I rummage through my pocket book and flip open my cell phone to call 911 but it says, "No Service." That damn cell phone tower must not be fixed yet. I go into Nicole's room to use the landline, but it's dead too. Go figure.

I decide to get help from Nicole's next-door-neighbor, the nice Chinaman. He's some kind of guru or witch doctor or something. I don't know if he still lives there or not.

His house is dark but there's a light on the front stoop where there's a big pile of junk. When I get closer I see soggy teddy bears, deflated balloons, lots of wet cards and letters, the ink all smeared. I pick up a few and find one I can read: "Dear Andy, may you rest in peace." This pile of junk is a shrine. Andy's dead and no help to me now, God bless him. I'm on my own.

I fight the wind to get back to Nicole's house. A gust nearly knocks me over. I've gotta get that girl out of here before Nicole comes home. Who knows how much time she has left? If I don't save her, I'll never forgive myself. I've already got enough blood on my hands, I don't need more.

# CHAPTER SIXTEEN

I find a small ax, I guess you'd call it a hatchet, on Nicole's deck and I'm hacking away at the bedroom door, until the wood starts to splinter. I don't know where my strength comes from, but you always hear those stories about mothers who lift up cars to free their trapped children, and I think it must be the adrenaline. Takes me a good fifteen minutes but I'm finally able to make a big enough hole in the door for me to climb through. I wipe off the splinters and sawdust and put down the hatchet. That's when I get a good look at what's in front of me.

Oh dear God. I barely recognize Devon as the pretty gal I've seen on TV and in magazines. I got no idea if she's dead or alive because her eyes are closed and her face is white as a ghost, her cheeks all sunken in. I walk over to the bed and see the dark circles under her eyes. Her lips are parched real bad and she's bone thin. I take her wrist and check to see if she's got a pulse. She does. I find a plastic water pitcher but it's empty.

I climb through the hole in the door and go downstairs to the kitchen. I fill up the pitcher with water and grab a straw on the counter. Not much in the fridge, but I find a half-empty jar of peanut butter, so I grab that and a spoon, and head back upstairs.

"Devon," I say to her. "I'm Pearl. Nikki's mom. I'm here to help you.

You're going to be okay, you hear me?" She just lies there.

"Here, let me give you some water, okay? Water?" I pull her up so she's in more of a sitting position. It's not hard to do—she's like a rag doll. I stick the straw in the pitcher and put the other end in her mouth. She doesn't seem to have enough strength to suck so I take the straw out of her mouth and pour the water in, real careful, straight from the pitcher. She swallows some, and gurgles, and the rest of it spills down her chin. I have no tissue to wipe it up. I try again—this time more goes down her throat. Her eyes flutter open.

"More," she says, her voice all raspy. I pour more water down her throat, little by little until she drinks almost half the pitcher. Like magic, it gives her energy. It's a wonder what a little water can do. Her eyes open all the way and she sits up some more. She licks her lips and says in a dry, croaky voice, "more water."

"You want more water? You got it, honey," I say and feed her more. "You want something to eat?" I ask and she nods her head. I spoon out some peanut butter and feed it to her. She eats it like it's going out of style, so I give her another spoonful, then some more water. I'm about to feed her more peanut butter, but she turns her head away—she's had enough, still licking her lips. She opens her mouth and says a little louder than before, "Who are you?"

"Pearl," I tell her. "I'm Nikki's mom." Then she asks, "where am I?" and I almost start to cry. "You're in Nikki's house. Nikki? You've been living here for a while. Do you remember?"

She looks around and slowly nods her head yes. "I remember," she says. "I thought I was dreaming." She's strong enough now and she reaches out for the pitcher and drinks the rest of the water all by herself.

"Andy," she says. "Is Andy dead or did I dream that?"

I don't want to upset her, but I figure it's best to tell the truth. "He's dead," I say. Bad idea—Devon starts weeping. Once she starts, she can't stop. "Shhhhh—stop your crying. You'll just make yourself sick."

"Nikki killed him. I saw her."

Now *I* feel like crying. And I never even knew the man.

Devon looks at me and I can see there's now some life in her eyes. "She's trying to kill me too. She's sick, Pearl. She's dangerous."

"I know, sweetheart, that's why I'm here. We gotta get you outta here before she comes back. I'm just not sure how. I can't carry you down a flight of stairs, I know that, and you can't make it on your own. I need to call 911 so we can get you to the hospital, but cell phones aren't working up here. Where's a land line I can use?"

"The country store," she says. "Bottom of the hill."

"Right." I look at my watch. Nicole's still on the air. As I'm about to leave, Devon stops me in my tracks with a single word... "Julia."

I'm not sure I heard her right. "What did you say?"

"Julia. Did Nikki kill her too?"

I nod my head and try not to break down.

"I don't think she meant to kill her," I say. I go back to the bed and sit beside Devon. "But when Nikki's career hit the skids, she started making Julia sick. Poisoning her. She even had the doctors believing Julia had some sort of disease. She liked the attention—all the doctors and nurses, the tests, the clinics and hospitals. And she got more attention by going on all them talk shows, sharing all the gory details. She was shameless. Shameless."

Devon looks more alert. She's listening carefully to what I say.

"I knew what Nikki was doing. Maybe not consciously, but I knew. Somewhere in my heart I suspected. T.J. did too. That's her husband. He killed himself two months after Julia passed. They said he overdosed, accidentally, but that's not what I think. I think it was on purpose. He couldn't live with himself."

I'm about to leave, but something about Devon makes me stay. I have more to get off my chest, things I've never told anybody, except Frank. I take Devon's dry hand in mine, but can't look her in the eyes. I stare down at the blanket.

"I couldn't let myself believe it could be true. That I gave birth to a monster. How can a mother, any mother, believe that about her daughter? So I did nothing. Put it out of my mind. And every day my granddaughter grew sicker, I cashed a paycheck, managing Nikki's pathetic career. I prayed Julia would get better—oh, did I do a lot of praying. But she needed more than prayers, that's for sure."

I look at Devon's face. I'm not sure how much she's getting, if her head's clear or not.

"Go on," she says.

"Nikki's not the only monster. When Julia died, Nikki paid her doctor nearly everything she had to look the other way." I pull my hand away from hers. "And, then there's me."

"You're not a monster," Devon says, all raspy again. "Monsters don't feel remorse."

"Oh, I feel remorse all right. Tried to off myself a few times. Sometimes I think the reason I can't manage to kill myself is because I know living is the real hell. Living is the best punishment for me. It's what I deserve."

"Or maybe..." Devon says, "you were spared...so you could help me."

"And that's just what I'm going to do, honey." I look at my watch and see Nicole's show is almost over. I get up from the bed. "I better hurry."

"Pearl," Devon says. "Thank you."

"Don't thank me yet. There'll be plenty of time for that once we get you to a hospital."

• • •

The storm's worse. The sky is dark. If you didn't know better you'd think it was nighttime, not the middle of the afternoon. I get drenched just getting back into my car.

I wind around the canyon's curves real slow, gripping the steering wheel tight. Can't hardly see out of my windshield. There's a stream of water flowing downhill that's getting stronger. It's so deep, it's like I'm wading in a river.

I'm on Kirkwood heading downhill toward Laurel Canyon Boulevard where that country store is. The road is steep as all get-out and my car starts sliding this way and that. "Don't panic, Pearl," I say to myself out loud. I press down on the brakes, but that just makes the car skid more.

I can never remember which way to turn the wheel when that happens—toward the skid or away from it. Toward I think, so I turn my wheel to the right but can't get any traction, what with the current and all. And now my car is hydroplaning, I think they call it. I slam on my brakes, but that's exactly what I'm *not* supposed to do. The car spins around like a carnival ride. I hold on tight to the steering wheel, but I'm completely losing control of the car. It keeps spinning until the rear end, where the gas tank is, crashes into a telephone pole.

"Ow!" I yell as my head hits the steering wheel on the rebound. Frank's car's so old it doesn't have airbags. My forehead's bleeding and I feel blood dripping down my face—I wipe it with my sleeve. But I got worse problems to worry about. Holy Christ—the fuel tank's on fire and it's spreading to the back seat. I jump out of the car and feel the water rushing at my ankles. I move away real quick, thinking the car might explode, but I slip and fall on the wet concrete. I look up and see the country store a good hundred yards ahead of me. Two young fellas, who are laying sandbags down are looking my way—they musta heard the crash.

A car on Laurel Canyon turns left onto my street, practically blinding me with its lights. I wave my arms like a crazy person to make myself seen so I don't get hit, but it doesn't matter because whoever's driving can see my car on fire right behind me.

The driver slows to a stop, right in the middle of the street. She gets out of the car to help me and that's when I see—it's Nicole. When she sees it's me, her mouth drops open. Me and her stare at each other like two animals—me on the ground, her standing in front of me, both of us getting battered by the wind and rain.

"Nicole!" I say, because nothing else comes to me. She just stands there, looking at me. There's evil in her eyes—I got no other way of putting it, and I know I'm going to die here in this storm, on this wet road. Nicole gets back in her car and starts it up. I scramble to my feet and try to get myself over to the right side of the road. She guns the engine and comes barreling right at me. I scream.

# *DEVON*

# CHAPTER SEVENTEEN

Thank God for Pearl. I don't know how close I came to dying—it's too scary to even think about—but if she makes it to the country store okay and an ambulance comes for me, I think I'll at least make it to the hospital alive. I'm still in extreme pain, but at least now I can think straight. I never thought I'd be so grateful to be able to simply lift my arm, but then who could've predicted I'd be held captive by a CSGB in the first place? I'm feeling stronger than I have since Nikki locked me in here.

Because Nikki feeds me so sporadically, when the mood strikes her, I can't keep track of time. It's difficult to figure out how long I've been here. Days? Weeks? I have no idea.

I don't know what Nikki's specific plan is, but I'm pretty sure killing me is on her "to do" list. There's no way she can let me live now, not with what I know.

I wish I understood her mental illness better—I honestly don't know if she's fully conscious of the evil things she's done or if her depraved mind has a way of reinventing things so she can live with herself. Maybe she's psychotic enough to actually believe Julia died of a terminal disease, that coyotes killed Wheezer, and that Andy's cat electrocuted him. And that she's rescued me from drug abuse and is now trying to rescue me from anorexia. But I can't rule out her cleverness—the way she's carefully documenting my deterioration on her radio show so if and when my organs shut down it won't come as a surprise to anyone and she'll be free of blame.

Any minute someone is going to crawl through my door—it could be the paramedics or it could be Nikki.

• • •

It's Nikki. I hear her bounding up the steps, calling my name. "Devon? Are you all right?" then, "Holy shit!" when she sees the busted door. She crawls through the hole, leaving puddles of water on the floor; she's soaking wet from the storm.

"What the hell's going on here?" she asks as she removes her raincoat and throws it on the floor.

"Oh, Nikki, I am *so* glad to see you." I'm saying anything I can think of to placate her. If I can avoid provoking her in any way, I'll be safe until the paramedics arrive. Pearl must have made it to the country store by now and help should be on the way. Nikki walks around the room, inspecting it.

"Who broke the fucking door?" she asks.

"Your mother. She wanted to take me with her, but I wouldn't go."

"Because?"

"Because...I want to stay with you." Nikki stops pacing, looks at me quizzically.

"Because?"

"Because I need you. To help me get well. I feel like an idiot, not trusting you. You've always had my best interest at heart, but I was too screwed up to appreciate it. I'm so ashamed. And I'm so sorry."

Nikki steps into the adjoining bathroom to get a towel and comes back into the room drying her hair.

"You're sorry?"

"*Really* sorry. I don't know how I can ever thank you for what you've done."

"I'm not buying it, Devon. The sweet talk. You said some pretty ugly things to me before I left." She tosses the towel towards the bathroom. "Why the sudden change of heart?"

"I was hungry, Nikki. I couldn't think straight. I realize now it was just part of your tough love—the same love that got me through detox. I couldn't see that then, but I can now." Nikki takes this in. I think she's starting to buy it.

"How can I trust you? How do I know you won't spread lies about me once you're better?"

"What lies?"

"Don't play dumb. We both know what lies. Andy Chiu for one. You said I killed him when we both know that's not true." I concentrate hard, striving to be both psychiatrist and actor at the same time—trying to get into her aberrant brain and figure out what she needs to hear. And make her believe it.

"You're right. Ever since the acid trip, I've been having flashbacks. Horrible images come to me out of nowhere. And then they vanish. It's really scary. I thought I saw you drop the CD player in Andy's Jacuzzi, but now I realize how ludicrous that is. You would never do anything that insane." Nikki sits down at the end of the bed. I'm making inroads.

"Acid does that, I know from experience," she says. "You may get more flashbacks for months to come."

"And if I do, I hope you'll be there to comfort me, to talk me down." Nikki nods her head. I keep on, building momentum. "You cared for me when no one else would. Please, believe me, Nikki, I need you."

Nikki sees the water pitcher, the peanut butter.

"Looks like Mother-fucking-Teresa beat me to the punch," she says.

I let out a laugh. "Nobody can make me laugh like you do, Nikki."

She laughs too. "After all those years on a goddamn sitcom, I better be able to reel off a few decent one-liners once in a while." She looks at me, still not sure whether or not to believe my turnaround.

"Come over here, Nikki. Please." We look at each other: two women, two addicts, two actors. We make quite a duo, a marriage made in hell, each complementing the other in the most destructive way possible. In a way, we deserve each other.

I can't look away or I'm sure to lose my audience. "Nikki, I need you," I say with all the conviction I can dredge up. "I need you to hold me."

Nikki crawls across the bed and lies down to the left of me. She turns my body away from her and spoons me, as if we were lovers. I close my eyes tight, knowing I need to be with her this way, this close, but feeling petrified at being in such proximity to evil.

"Don't leave me, Nikki. I want things to be the way they used to be. Just you and me. Like mother and child."

Nikki tenses, suddenly sits up. "What's *that* supposed to mean?"

"What?"

"Mother and child? *Really?*"

"You said it yourself—that I'm like a daughter to you. That's all I meant."

"What the hell did my lying son-of-a-bitch mother tell you?"

"Nothing! I don't know what you're talking about!"

"Julia! That's what!"

"What about her?"

"Oh, the dumb act again. I knew I couldn't trust you. I'm sure you got quite an earful from that fucking bitch."

"No! She didn't say anything, really!" Now I'm scared. Nikki's turned into someone else. She looks manic, her eyes darting about the room.

"You think Pearl's so badass, do you? That she's going to send help to rescue you? Well I got news for you. She's dead."

Oh God. "What? What do you mean? I just saw her."

"She had an accident on the way down the hill. Her car smashed into a pole and just blew up. When she managed to get out, she got hit by a car. I witnessed the whole thing. So tragic."

I don't know whether to believe her or not. But I can't help it, I start crying.

"Oh, you cry for her, but when have you, or anyone else for that matter, ever shed a tear for me?"

She picks up a pillow. "It's time," she says. "Yeah, it's time."

Nikki leans over me, places the pillow on my face and holds it there. I grab at the air, thrashing and squirming. I manage to get my hands around her throat and squeeze hard, feeling her larynx beneath my thumbs. She makes strangling choking sounds but doesn't let up. She's stronger than me and my fingers seem to have little effect on her. She presses the pillow more tightly against my nose and mouth, snarling and grunting like a diseased animal. The lack of oxygen is making me woozy, weak. I will not die, I tell myself. I will not die.

I continue squeezing Nikki's neck with my left hand as my right reaches for the hatchet I've hidden under the covers. I grip it as tightly as I can, then slowly bring it out. I've only got one chance to get this right.

I feel a surge of strength as I swing my arm up and bring the blade down hard, striking Nikki in the back. She screams, "Devon!" and I hear the sickening sound the hatchet makes as it slices into her flesh. Nikki stares at me with the hurt look of someone who's been betrayed. After a moment, her body goes limp, collapsing on top of me.

I push the pillow off my face and gasp for breath. I'm stuck beneath her, her face pressed against mine, blood starting to soak us both. I can't tell if she's dead or alive, I just know she's unable to move.

We're both going to die here. All my strength is gone. I pant like a weightlifter but find it hard to breathe with Nikki's dead weight on me. The news mentioned it's a Friday so Nikki isn't expected to show up at the radio station until next week. That means no one will look for her until Monday afternoon. And no one will look for me. Andy's dead. Pearl is most likely dead. Trey thinks I'm in Wisconsin. I'll never survive three days without water. If I had the strength to cry, I would. For Andy and Pearl. For Julia. For Wheezer. And yeah, even for the wretch who brought all this devastation upon us, poor sick Nikki.

# CHAPTER EIGHTEEN

" but I heard him exclaim as he drove out of sight, 'Merry Christmas ... **b** to all, and to all a good night.'"

"Oh, honey, that was wonderful."

"I memorized the whole thing."

"You did! Come here, Devy. Let mommy and I give you a big hug and lots of kisses."

# CHAPTER NINETEEN

"Jesus Christ!" Someone's slapping my face. My eyes open but my vision is blurred.

"Devon! It's me, Trey!" I feel him lift Nikki and place her next to me, on her stomach. I suck in the precious air, feeling relief from the pressure on my chest.

"Oh my God," he's saying to himself, looking at all the blood, not knowing where it's coming from. "Oh my God, oh my God."

"I think I killed her," I try to say but I don't think he can hear me; there's not much left of my voice.

Someone enters the room; I can feel the heavy footsteps. "Sir, step away from the bodies," a stern voice says. "You have to leave. This is a crime scene."

"You're going to be okay," says Trey, crying as he leaves. "You're going to be okay."

I can see them carrying Nikki out on a stretcher. She's on her stomach, the hatchet still embedded in her back. Her face is turned towards me. Her eyes are open and we look at each other for a moment. I still have no idea if she's dead or alive, conscious or not, but her face bears the same twisted expression as the one on the cardboard standee that appeared in my nightmare.

# CHAPTER TWENTY

There's a warm hand on my shoulder, gently shaking me awake. "Sorry to wake you, Ms. O'Keefe, but I wanted to chat with you today about your condition. I'm Dr. Schiff."

I yawn, and as I cover my mouth, I see the IV that's piercing the back of my hand. I also notice a fresh cast on my leg. I'm surrounded by sage green walls. The color is supposed to be soothing, but it just reminds me of the last time I was here at Cedars and I find it depressing.

"How are you feeling today?" the doctor asks.

"Numb."

"That doesn't surprise me. You're in shock, which given what you've been through, is a perfectly normal reaction."

"How is Nikki?"

"I'm afraid I can't discuss other patients with you," he says after a long pause.

"So she's alive?" Another pause.

"As I said, I—"

"Right, I know. But can you just tell me if—"

"Let's talk about *you*, Devon. Your vitals are creeping into the normal range, but you're not healing well at all." He looks at his clipboard. "In fact, the injuries you sustained in your accident are actually worse now than when you were last here. What have you been doing, skiing? Mud wrestling?"

"Just trying to stay alive, doc. It's a long story. I'm sure it'll be made into a very bad movie someday."

"Well, whatever you did it was enough to extend the healing period for another couple of months." He looks again at his chart. "But the good news is your pelvic fracture is stable and there's no infection or damage to your nerves, just the muscles surrounding the pelvis. You'll probably walk with a limp for a few months but all in all, you're very lucky. How's the pain?" he asks. "On a scale of one to ten."

I think back on how I felt the day I investigated the house—my pain was an eleven. "I'd say about an eight."

"We can get you on some painkillers," Dr. Schiff says. "Perhaps a morphine drip."

"Actually, can I try to get through this without drugs?" After what I've been through, I want to be in complete control of my body and mind.

"Your choice," he says. "You're going to need quite a bit of physical therapy, though. I'm also sending someone down from Psych to talk to you.

"Psych? Why?"

"I understand you've been held captive, no?"

"Yes," I say, feeling, of all things, embarrassed.

"Your mother's been called. She'll be here this afternoon. I assume she'll care for you once you're released?"

"I guess." I picture myself lying in bed at the Oakwood, my mom out on the town, looking for some new Beverly Hills suitor.

"You're going to need a lot of care. And don't be afraid to pig out. I've prescribed a high-calorie, high-fat diet to get some meat back on those bones. I know your Hollywood producers may tell you otherwise, but trust me, the sunken cheeks are not a good look on you. I'll see you tomorrow." He gives my toes a squeeze, then stands there for a moment, looking uncomfortable. "Do you feel up to talking to the police now?"

"The police?"

"They're waiting to speak with you. About the attempted murder."

"Oh. You mean Nikki trying to smother me."

"Uh, no. They're referring to your striking her with a hatchet."

"Oh, that," I say, wondering how much worse things can get.

• • •

Two detectives enter my room and read me my Miranda rights. I may be in shock, but I have enough wits about me to know better than to speak to them without a lawyer present as I'm sure they had hoped. I do have some experience with the law, having been arrested for shoplifting, DUI, and possession of narcotics—the obligatory crimes of all card-carrying members of CSGB. They agree to come back tomorrow when my attorney will be present. Before they leave, I ask them when I'll be able to see Trey. Not until we've both been interviewed, they tell me. Separately.

I imagine how this latest episode will play itself out. Two crazy actresses found bloody in bed together, one with a hatchet in her back. Doesn't get much more lurid than that.

I can easily predict the sensationalistic headline: BANSHEE DOES HATCHET JOB ON FORMER SITCOM ACTRESS. I make a promise to myself not to surf the Internet, read the tabloids or watch the news. Who knows what people will believe. Why torture myself?

• • •

"I got this at the gift shop. I thought it might cheer you up," my mom says as she enters my room. She hands me, of all things, a plastic snow globe. I shake it and the snow falls on the Hollywood sign like it never would in real life. I set it on the nightstand.

She kisses me on the forehead, then pulls a chair over to my bedside, a smug 'cat that ate the canary' look on her face.

"I have some good news, honey. All kinds of offers are pouring in. I just spoke to a producer who wants you to do a reality show. Really emotional stuff— how you're coping with everything after your imprisonment, your psycho-therapy, our relationship—the whole shebang. It could be at least two seasons, they said, especially if there's a trial for Nikki."

"So she's alive?"

"Of course she's alive. I didn't raise a murderer. So, what do you think? Another TV series sure would help cover any medical bills your insurance won't pay. Better yet, it would keep you in the public eye."

Had I not realized it before, it's clear to me now why I began using drugs and alcohol in the first place. In my most calm, parental voice I speak to my mother like the child she is.

"I'm tired, mom. I need rest."

"Okay, honey. You rest and think about it. We can talk later. It's all very exciting."

Before she turns to leave, I ask, "Did you call my attorney?"

"No, not yet."

"Mom, you have to call her. It's very important. I can't talk to the police until she comes."

"All right, there's nothing to get upset about. You didn't do anything illegal. I'm sure they know that."

"All they know is that I struck Nikki in the back with a hatchet. I could go to prison for that."

"Don't be silly, honey. It'll all get straightened out."

"Do you have my attorney's number?"

"I think so. It's Hollis Shawn, right?"

"Shawn Holley. Call her now."

• • •

I wish Trey were here to take a picture of the unusual tableaux in my hospital room. Seated in a semi-circle around my bed are the two detectives—one female, Sergeant Reese, and one male, Sergeant Howells—Shawn Holley, and my mom. I tell my story from beginning to end, clear-eyed, unemotional, just the facts, ma'am. I want them to see I'm not an hysterical, out-of-control druggie, but a credible young woman with an incredible story to tell.

"Based on your testimony," Sergeant Howells says, "we'll reopen the Andy Chiu investigation, now that there's a feasible motive for homicide. There's no statute of limitations in California, so we can also investigate the death of Julia Colton."

"I'm familiar with Munchausen-by-Proxy syndrome," Sergeant Reese says. "I uncovered a case in Hancock Park a few years back. Again, it helps provide a motive for Nikki's behavior. And we'll be talking to this Pierce fellow you mentioned. Always good to get one more drug dealer off the streets."

As they get up to leave, Sergeant Howells says, "My daughter is a fanshee. Do you think...?" He smiles weakly and takes out a note pad and pen.

My mom stands up, takes them from him and hands them to me. "Of course—she'd be glad to. What's her name?"

Shawn and I exchange looks. She handles a lot of celebrities but this sort of thing still sickens her.

"Cynthia," he says.

I'm appalled, but I give him the autograph just the same, wondering if my signature will be more or less valuable if I'm a convicted felon. Detective Reese takes a less warm and fuzzy approach: "Don't leave town without first notifying us," she says. "Depending on our investigation you could still be arrested for assault or attempted murder."

Shawn can't resist a little sarcasm. Pointing to me in a cast and IV, she asks, "Does it look like she's planning on taking a trip to Fiji any time soon?"

"We can't be too careful, ma'am," she says. "It's happened before."

• • •

A couple hours later, Trey enters carrying a vase of yellow tulips.

"Please, don't get up," he jokes. "Just say, thank you, they're beautiful."

"Thank you, they're beautiful."

He sets the vase on the empty windowsill. No other flowers help brighten up the room. No gifts of any kind for that matter. Apparently, even my fans are a bit tentative about comforting me after what they've heard.

Trey sits on my bed, leans over and puts his arms around me as gently as he can. We hold each other for a long time, neither of us speaking. When we part, we both reach for the Kleenex box at the same time, which makes us laugh for a moment.

"You're going to be okay," Trey says, wiping his eyes.

*No. I'm never going to be okay. But I'm an actor. I can act okay.*

"Of course," I lie.

"You look wiped out. You sure you want me to stay?"

"Yes. But I'm warning you—my mom's just left, so you might get a dose of residual bitchiness from me."

"You could never be a bitch," he says, then adds, "although remind me never to argue with you when there's a hatchet around."

"Ah, yes, the inconvenient hatchet."

"Somebody's got some 'splainin' to do," he says and I almost laugh but manage to stop myself as it would hurt too much. "Whenever you're ready," he adds. "Doesn't have to be now."

"No, now's okay. I want to tell you everything." And I do. Everything from Wheezer to Pierce to Andy, to Pearl and Julia, to the aforementioned hatchet in the back. And suddenly the memory of discovering the TMZ footage on Nikki's phone floats back into my consciousness. Trey doesn't interrupt once, just lets me tell the whole abhorrent story in one long extended breath.

"I wish I'd known what was going on. I wish I'd been there to protect you," he says when I've finished.

"It's not your fault. Now I want to hear your story. I'm still a little worried. What did you tell the cops?"

"The first thing was what Nikki told me weeks ago. That you were in Wisconsin. That there was no way I could reach you."

"Good," I nod. "That's good."

"Then I told them about the night at the Viper Room. How it was Nikki who gave you the cranberry juice and how I suspected she was the one who spiked it with acid."

"Even better. What happened yesterday? How did you manage to show up at the house? Start from the beginning. I want to hear everything."

"I was outside with Wassim, laying down some sandbags 'cause the store was starting to flood. Then we heard a loud crash. We looked up and saw the flash flood had caused a car to spin into a metal pole. There were sparks and then the back end went up in flames. I tried calling 911, but my phone wouldn't work—the cell tower was down. So Wassim ran inside to use the landline. That's when I saw an old lady—she must have been about seventy—get out of the car."

"Pearl. Nikki's mom."

"Right, Pearl. The wind knocked her down. I waited for the light to change so I could cross the crowded boulevard and help her. But before I could reach her, I saw your Mini Cooper turn onto Kirkwood from Laurel and just stop in the middle of the freakin' street. And then I saw Nikki get out. I could tell it was her—she wasn't even wearing a coat or a hat or anything—she was just standing there, getting drenched, having a stare-down with the old lady."

Trey grabs a cup of water from my tray and takes a sip. I can tell he's upset retelling the story.

"You sure you want to hear all this?" he asks.

"Yes."

"Nikki floored it, man, just floored it. She plowed down her mother, but that's not all. After she crashed into her, she backed up and floored it again. Ran right over her. I couldn't believe what I was seeing."

I wince.

"Wassim saw some of it too—he came out of the store after he called 911. I'm sure they can match the tire treads on her body with the treads on the car."

"Go on."

"Nikki took off up the hill and I checked out Pearl to see if she was alive, but of course she wasn't. It was the most gruesome thing I've ever seen—her body was, well, you don't need to know the details, but the weird thing is, her face; she looked at peace. Almost like she was smiling."

I nod, remembering my conversation with her last night. "So anyway," Trey continues, "I ran back into the store and called 911 to give them Nikki's address. Then I started to piece things together. Your acid trip, Nikki telling me you went back to Wisconsin. And I began to wonder about you. I just had a bad feeling. I knew something was wrong. I knew you'd be in that house, that creepy-ass house." He caresses my hand, then gives it a loving squeeze.

"You know the rest. The police, the paramedics. Did they tell you about Nikki?"

"No, nothing."

"Huh," Trey says. He's holding something back.

"What? You can tell me." He hesitates.

"She's... paralyzed from the waist down. Her spinal cord was severed."

"Oh God."

"Don't you dare feel guilty, Devon. That freak tried to smother you to death. You saved your own life."

"I know. But what do you think will happen to her?"

"My mom says she could be arrested for first degree murder and possibly false imprisonment, depending how the investigation goes. But I saw online that Nikki's attorney said you tried to kill her because you were having an acid flashback. That you thought she was the devil."

"So it's my word against hers."

"Pretty much. My mom says it could go either way. I think we both know that justice isn't something to take for granted in this town. You know about the Dion Jackson case?"

"The guy who was beaten to death by the police."

"My cousin. A college student just like me. He was pulled over in

Brentwood for 'driving while black.' It was captured on video, but the cops got off."

"I'm sorry."

"I just bring it up because you need to get a really good attorney."

"I have one. But so does Nikki. First degree murder, huh? She could spend the rest of her life in jail."

"Yeah. Then the worst she could do is run over small rodents with her wheelchair. She'd be bored stiff."

"You're a sick man," I say, grateful for a little gallows humor given everything that's transpired.

"And you're a sick woman. We make a good pair." Trey leans over and kisses me on the lips.

"Our first consensual kiss," I say to him, "and it's in a hospital. How romantic. What a great story to tell our children. Our hypothetical children."

# CHAPTER TWENTY-ONE

Nighttime is the worst. More often than not, I awake shaking after experiencing the most horrific nightmares you can imagine. Most of them involve Nikki, although sometimes she doesn't actually appear as herself. But I know the zombies and demons, the beasts that lunge at me, are all her.

Last night I dreamt I was back home with my mom. The doorbell rang and when I answered it, I was greeted by Andy, his body burnt to a crisp, his eyes hanging out of their sockets. In some of the dreams I'm being smothered; I wake up gasping for breath. I've thrown out my pillows—can't bear to even look at one without feeling a chill. Now when I sleep, I rest my head on a rolled-up bath towel.

It's been months since I left the hospital. I'm renting a studio apartment in West Hollywood, living off the severance I received from *Banshee*. My SAG health insurance covers my daily caregiver, the invaluable Ligaya who brings me kalamay, a sticky green rice dessert from Filipinotown in Echo Park. Ligaya is especially good at dealing with the press and paparazzi. She's as protective as a mama bear; you don't want to cross her. I'm able to make it to my twelve-step meetings and therapy sessions, both physical and psychological, without a single photo showing up online or in the tabloids—or so I'm told. Ligaya's clever with disguises and has provided me with hilarious wigs to wear when we go out. My favorite is the Esperanza Spalding doo.

I sent my mother back to Kenosha with an, "I love you, Mom, but you're not healthy for me right now," after we got into a huge argument about my not wanting to do the reality show. When I sent her packing, she broke down. I knew I should console her, but I couldn't bring myself to say the appropriate words, so she left on a not-so-good note.

The producers kept contacting me and my agent to the point where I felt like maybe I needed a restraining order to get them off my back. But I kept refusing to speak with them and eventually they went away. I should add my new agent was also pissed at me. I fired his ass.

The whole episode upset me, but not enough to drive me back to drugs or alcohol. In fact, I've been abstinent for five months, two weeks, and three days. I'd be lying if I said it's been easy. I'm not at peace.

I have an appointment with my psychiatrist, Dr. Buzzelli, who I've been seeing twice a week for the past couple of months. I was referred to her by Dr. Schiff, who felt I needed treatment for the depression and anxiety that set in following the trauma I experienced.

I don my latest disguise: baggy pants and a Spongebob sweatshirt, accessorized with a floppy hat and Garbo sunglasses. As I walk to my car, I'm aware of the limp in my left leg, which my physical therapist thinks will probably go away by the time *Day of the Locust* opens in a month. The thought of being on stage again terrifies me, but then just about everything frightens me these days—loud noises, cars I'm sure are following me, strangers I pass on the street.

But I feel safe sipping herbal tea on Dr. Buzzelli's couch. She's a genuine nurturer, much like Nikki in the early days but without the side dish of psycho. Like therapists I've had in the past, she wears large jewelry and artsy clothes. Her voice is comforting and she has an uncanny ability to tune in to what I'm saying and feeling.

We sit in silence for a few minutes. Doctor B never starts the conversation; she waits for me to speak. I tell her how yesterday I visited the

Westwood Memorial Park and Mortuary. In the Corridor of Memories is a modest marker on one of the white mausoleum crypts. It reads, "Marilyn Monroe: 1926-1962." The plaque stands out from the others because it's the only dark one, the result of fans leaving lip-sticked kisses on it for decades. What a loss, I thought. Marilyn was just coming into her own as an actor, but her demons got the best of her. She swallowed forty barbiturates. There are conspiracy theories claiming she was murdered, but I prefer to believe she took her own life. Somehow this would make her less of a victim. From what I've read, suicide was her best option, the only way she could escape from herself—her fears, her pain, her loneliness. Andy told me to trust my instincts and I wonder, what if Marilyn was trusting hers when she downed those pills?

"I was in a dark mood," I tell Doctor B. "And I almost left. But I forced myself to walk further down the hall and do what I came to do: say goodbye to Andy." I stop talking. I know what's coming and I don't yet have the strength to continue.

Finally, Dr. B comments, "And did you?"

"Yes. I ran my hand over the plaque and said goodbye." I stop speaking again. My breathing and pulse speed up and I feel the "fight or flight" response. I pick up my mug and feel it's warmth on my palms. I take a sip of tea. Doctor B can see my hand shaking.

"Are you all right, Devon?" she asks, leaning forward. I shake my head no and stare down at the rug, getting lost in its patterns.

After a long period of silence, Doctor B asks, "Tell me what happened next."

"After I said goodbye to Andy, I anticipated breaking down and wailing on the marble floor like the banshee I am."

"But you didn't?"

"No."

I take a moment to consider whether or not to tell Dr. B what came next. My first thought is to lie but that'd be breaking a twelve-step rule and that shit's over. But omission isn't really lying. I could just continue with my narrative, leaving out the most important part, the part I dread speaking aloud, but that's why I'm here—to confront the difficult issues in my life and try to make sense of them so I don't make the same mistakes again.

I brace myself and decide to answer Doctor B's question. I avoid her eyes, focusing instead on an abstract painting on the wall to the left of her head.

"I felt anger. It was pretty scary. I could feel it in my gut—that's where it started—then it sort of radiated throughout my body. I felt like I was going to internally combust and didn't know what to do. There were a few mourners in the hallway, quietly paying their respects, so I bolted for the bathroom. Thank God it was empty."

I look Doctor B in the eyes.

"I beat the shit out of myself."

She nods. "Go on."

"I pounded on my arms and legs. I scratched the inside of my arms until I drew blood, I pinched my nipples and pulled my hair. I kicked the wall as hard as I could, first with one foot, then the other, until my toes ached. I punched myself so hard in the stomach that I threw up. But I didn't cry. I cleaned myself up at the sink, dried myself with a few paper towels and drove home."

"Did that make you feel better?"

"No. I'm still carrying around that rage and I don't know what to do with it."

"Do you know what the source of your anger is?"

"Of course. Andy. I killed him."

Doctor B looks confused. "I'm sorry, I don't understand. Nikki killed him. You tried to save him but weren't able to."

"No. I made a stupid, stupid mistake that cost him his life. He wanted to take me out of Nikki's house, but I wouldn't let him. I think I was trying to prove something to myself. That I didn't need anyone's help, that I was strong. I thought I had a plan to save myself, but it was ridiculous. And now he's dead. And Pearl's dead too. Both of them would be alive if I hadn't made such a spectacularly poor choice that day. I don't know how to live with myself." I bite my lip and hang my head, too ashamed to look at the doctor.

"I wish I could offer up some sort of bromide to make you feel better, Devon. But healing takes time."

Shit. I wanted a quick fix. I don't know how much longer I can suffer this guilt without doing something horrible to make it go away.

"Can you please look at me for a moment?" Doctor B asks.

I raise my head.

"I want to give you something to think about. You used the word 'stupid' to describe your actions. I'm asking you to stop that."

"But—"

"Listen to me. You were in the middle of the kind of trauma very few people experience. A person with a severe mental illness was making you sick. You were being tortured, held against your will. You weren't capable of making any kind of rational decision. No one would be."

I try to digest what she's saying, but I can't let go of my guilt.

Doctor Buzzelli's voice is stern. "Devon, look at me."

I realize my head is hanging low again. I straighten up.

"Sorry. I heard what you said and I'll give it some thought."

"Thank you. There's one more thing I want you to hear."

*No, I've heard enough. I want to go home.*

"We both know there's been self-abuse in your past. You've intentionally caused yourself physical pain."

"I know, haven't we been through that already?"

"Yes, but what I want you to know is that not all self-harm is physical, nor is self-harm always conscious. Sometimes people bring great damage to themselves when they think they're doing the opposite. Sometimes people commit slow suicide by a series of acts and inactions."

I put my mug down and close my eyes for a moment or two.

"I *wanted* to get myself killed?"

"I don't know. I can't tell you that. It would be glib of me to make such a diagnosis at this point. But it's something for us to work on here."

"Add it to the list," I say, picking up my mug for a badly needed gulp of tea.

"How are the nightmares? Still every night?"

I nod. "I can't control them."

"No, you can't. They're normal for what you've been through. I wish I could tell you they'll go away soon, but they may not."

Dr. B grabs a pen and a pad of paper from her end table and begins writing. "But let's try you on an alpha-blocker that's had some success with PTSD patients."

"I didn't know I had PTSD. Nikki—she just keeps on giving, huh?"

Dr. B smiles as she hands me the prescription.

"Thank you. Will I be able to get this filled when I'm in solitary confinement?"

Doctor B doesn't laugh. "When will you hear about your case?"

"Soon. My criminal defense attorney says I've got about a fifty-fifty chance they'll press charges and put me on trial. It's pretty hard to prove self-defense when the threatening weapon is a pillow and there's no other physical evidence."

"If anyone can turn something as comforting as a pillow into a weapon of destruction it's Nikki Barnes. But you survived, Devon. A lesser person would be dead."

• • •

"Hi, Devon. Shawn Holley here." Ligaya and I are outside Starbucks when we get her call. We take long walks these days; I'm trying to build up my muscles.

"Shawn! Do you have news for me?" Ligaya and I stop walking. I hold onto a parking meter for support; Ligaya plays with the cocker spaniel that's tied up below.

"Sure do," she says. "Nikki Barnes is under arrest for the murders of Pearl Barnes and Andy Chiu. She's being held without bail."

I exhale, suddenly realizing I've been holding my breath.

"Are you still there?" she asks.

"Yeah, yeah, I'm here. What else?"

"The detectives discovered Andy had hidden security cameras high up in the trees in his backyard. Apparently a few years ago he had problems with a stalker. There's grainy but discernible footage of Nikki dropping the CD player into the Jacuzzi, which confirms your testimony."

"Oh my God. And what about Pearl?"

"Tremaine's and Wassim Nazari's first-hand testimony of her murder along with the tire tread evidence pretty much clinched the deal. There'll be a trial, but I don't think you need to worry about Nikki getting off. It looks like an open and shut case to me."

"That's fantastic, Shawn, you're the best." Ligaya smiles at me—she knows I'm getting good news.

Hearing that Nikki is behind bars makes my body go limp—the tension just dissipates. Knowing she was somewhere out there made me fearful. Even though she's paralyzed and had no idea where I was living, I felt her presence hovering over my life everyday.

"But here's the best part, Devon," Shawn says, a smile in her voice. "The part I've been saving for last: there'll be no charges against you. Reese and Howells believe you struck Nikki in order to save your life."

After I finish my call with Shawn, I share the news with Ligaya.

"You're free, Palanggâ," she says.

"I am. Freedom's something I always took for granted. Never again."

"A couple of years ago, my cousin wrote an article that criticized Duterte's government. He was executed. I know about freedom."

I put my arm around her and we begin our walk home.

# CHAPTER TWENTY-TWO

The first time Trey and I made love, I began crying and couldn't stop. Believe it or not, I had never had sex with someone while sober, but more importantly, never with someone I truly cared for and who cared for me.

"Hey, hey, what's goin' on?" he asked in a tender voice, stopping all movement. "You're not a banshee anymore, why the tears?"

"Don't stop," I said, but he did since I was still crying. We held each other for a long time until I was all cried out. We made love again and spent the rest of the night discovering the joys and secrets of each other's bodies.

I'm growing to love Trey—his maturity, his compassion, his sense of humor. He's so unlike other guys I've dated—no bad boy antics, just a healthy and loving presence in my life.

"I was thinking," he says to me in bed on a late Sunday morning, our bodies naked beneath the sheets. "After I get my Masters, there are a few PhD programs in Environmental Law I'm looking into. They're all on the east coast. So when your play moves to Off-Broadway—"

"*If* my play moves to Off-Broadway."

"—we could see each other without having to travel across the country."

I'm bowled over. No man's ever talked to me about a possible future together.

"There's a program at Syracuse that looks promising. Green Lakes State Park isn't far from there. We could do some hiking, silent or otherwise."

"Yeah," I say, "maybe."

"Or, if you prefer, we could split up and never see each other again."

I laugh. "No, no, I don't mean to sound blasé, it's just I have to give careful thought to how I want to live my life, post-Nikki. I was thinking that after the show closes, maybe I'd like to go to college and study psychology."

"You mean you'd give up show biz?"

"I'm not sure. I love acting, but it can be insular—I think it's time to give more thought to someone other than myself for a while. I just don't know yet what that might mean. Time is precious. The thought of working on another mediocre show isn't very appealing."

"*Mediocre?*"

"I'm sorry, I know you were a fanshee."

"Still am, babe. Always will be." He pulls me close and kisses my neck. "I'm sure there's more creatively fulfilling work out there. If you do keep acting, you'll just have to be discerning about which projects are worthy of your talent."

"Oh, so you think I'm talented, do you?"

"I do. But that's not why I love you."

"Did you just...?"

"I did."

"I thought so." We lie there for a while, not saying anything. I want to say "I love you" back but a thought is nagging at me.

"There's something I need to ask you," I finally say.

"Go for it."

"Nikki told me you've slept with every woman in Laurel Canyon. Is there any truth to that?"

There's a disconcerting pause, followed by a flat, "No."

"Okay, so maybe not *every* woman. Give me a number."

Another pause. "One," he says.

"Who was she, if I may ask."

This pause is so long, I slowly pull away from him.

"Nikki," he says.

"What?"

"It was only once. A few years ago."

I can't speak. My head feels like it's going to explode.

"Our delivery guy was out sick so I took a bag of groceries to her house. She sort of seduced me."

I sit up. "When were you planning on telling me this?"

"I don't know. I could never find the right moment."

I grab my robe, slipping into it as I get out of bed. I pull the cord on my Japanese paper blinds and look out the window.

"Get out," I say without looking at him.

"I was afraid you'd react this way. That's why I never told you. I didn't want to lose you."

He gets out of bed, comes up behind me and reaches for me. I pull away.

"Don't touch me. I'm so sickened right now, I can't even look at you."

He moves away and I can hear him putting on his clothes.

"I'm so sorry, Devon. I should've told you."

"Please get out."

"I'm going, I'm going," he says, zipping up his pants. I walk past him, into the bathroom. I turn the shower on and wait until the water gets hot, almost scalding. I scrub every inch of my body.

# CHAPTER TWENTY-THREE

I'm looking at my reflection in my dressing room mirror; platinum blonde Faye Greener stares back at me. In fifteen minutes, I'll be stepping onto the stage for the opening night of *Day of the Locust*. I'm nervous. I know my lines. I know my blocking. I know Faye inside out. But I'm concerned I won't be able to lose myself in her tonight for the ninety-nine people who have come to be entertained in our shoebox of a theatre.

My mind is a mess these days, but as Doctor Buzzelli predicted, it gets a little better everyday. The crying jags still hit me with the shock of a surprise party but they're less frequent. The nightmares are also tapering off. I pray my fragile mind won't let me down on stage tonight, that I won't go into a catatonic state under the footlights. Yes, I'm being overly dramatic. Weeks of being Faye Greener have affected me this way.

Nathanael West's *Day of the Locust* explored the perversity of Hollywood, the alienation of characters whose desire for success has failed to come true. I've seen this first-hand through Nikki and Pearl, and of course, my mom. But as we all know, desperation isn't limited to Hollywood. Many people aspire to live lives beyond their reach. I think of my dad whose failure to get his novel published ate away at him.

Nigel understands despair, which is why, I think, this production is so compelling. He visited me in the hospital one night, sneaking in after visiting hours. Away from the theatre, he let his guard down. We talked about our pasts, our childhoods.

"I grew up in abject poverty," he confided. "My family lived in a graffiti covered tower block in London's East End. My mum raised me and my four brothers and sisters on a schoolteacher's salary. Dad left when I was six." Suddenly, his penchant for throwing around erudite references in a posh accent made sense. Since that night, I consider Nigel a dear friend.

The stage manager cues me to take my place in the wings. Hugging the curtain, I sneak a peek at the audience. I know it will be a supportive one—the house is filled with people who care about me—Ligaya, my twelve-step program friends, Dr. Schiff, Dr. Buzzelli, and some of the cast and crew from *Beverly Hills Banshee*. My mom is seated next to Shane, who, not-so-coincidentally is the most famous person in the room; she touches his arm each time she comments on something she's read in the program. Missing, of course, is Trey. When I told my mom I broke things off with him, her response was classic: "He was sweet, Devon, but I'm sure you'll find someone else to take care of you."

"Yup," was all I was capable of.

• • •

When I step out onto the stage, there's immediate applause. I find this a little annoying; it's not like I've done anything yet to deserve it. The instantaneous clapping reminds me of those sitcoms where all an actor has to do is make an entrance and there's thunderous applause just for the joy they've brought audiences in the past. But I appreciate the acknowledgement of support for my real life trials—the fact that I'm here, sober, and weighing a healthy one hundred and twelve pounds; a special shout-out to Ben & Jerry's Boom Chocolatta for that.

The applause momentarily throws me, but I manage to get in character and stay there once I speak my first line of dialogue. By the time the curtain comes down and the audience rises to its feet, its appreciation is as meaningful to me as the applause I received when I shared for the first time at a meeting—when I announced I was sober for thirty days.

Even more satisfying is that the applause isn't just for me; it's for the whole ensemble. As I stand on the stage holding hands and bowing with the rest of the cast, it feels rewarding to be part of a whole, to create something as a team. Given who my mother is, this may be my only family. I'm hoping the theatre can continue to serve this function until the day comes when I'm ready to start one of my own.

I see tons of flowers as I enter my dressing room. I check out the cards and am touched that both friends and strangers wish me well. The most spectacular of the bunch is a vase of two dozen long-stemmed red roses. I read the card, which says simply, "Break a leg. Love, Trey." I miss him.

A stream of people has begun to flow into the room. Matteo, still dressed as Tod Hackett bends me over backwards and kisses me on the lips. "Cast party at the Viper Room!" he yells, releasing me from his grip. I shoot him a look of disbelief. "Kidding," he says.

"You were fabulous," my mom says, pushing her way through the crowd. She gives me a hug. "When will you know if they're taking the show to Broadway?"

"*Off-*Broadway, mom. And who knows. We have to see how well the show is received here first."

"What's to see?" she says. "The audience loved it."

"Of course they did. Most of them are friends of the cast. We have to see what the critics think."

"Well, I'd be thrilled if it went to New York. It could lead to bigger and better paying roles for you. Maybe get your beautiful face back on TV or even the movies, huh? And by the way," she adds, "there are *tons* of paparazzi out there." She says this as if it were a *good* thing.

This inane conversation is interrupted by Rick, the house manager, who enters holding a bud vase covered in red cellophane.

"One more," he says, handing it to me. I peel off the wrapping and see the vase holds a single black rose. The room goes quiet as everyone gets a look at it.

"Okayee," Rick says as he turns and leaves. I open the small envelope and remove the card.

"What's it say?" my mom asks.

I read the card to myself: "Lies are like stabs to the soul. They destroy you. Love, Nikki." I'm so startled, I drop the glass vase on the concrete floor, where it shatters. Nigel can see the card has upset me.

"Whoa!" he says, picking up pieces of the vase and placing them on the counter. Audrey enters the room, sees Nigel holding the flower.

"Is that rose *black?*" she asks innocently.

"Yes, someone please get rid of it this instant," Nigel barks, holding it out.

Matteo takes the rose from Nigel. "Ow! Those thorns are sharp!" he says. He holds his index finger up to his lips and licks off the blood.

# EPILOGUE

Merle Haggard is on the rental car radio on this overcast day as I drive through the San Joaquin Valley, smack dab in the middle of California. It's about a four-hour drive from LA to where I'm headed, but I don't mind the alone time. My depression is manageable these days—it's there pretty much every morning, but like June gloom, it dissipates by noon. The crying jags are gone but every so often jarring images flash in my brain like those "gotcha!" moments in slasher films.

I'm still having nightmares, which is why I've flown clear across the country from New York to be here. Closure. Everyone uses the word, but I have no idea what it means or how it will feel once I attain it, *if* I attain it.

Glancing down at the GPS, I see I'm only ten minutes from my destination. The fact that I'm gnawing on the knuckles of my free hand should've tipped me off. I place both hands on the steering wheel and grip it tight, trying to avoid 'catastrophizing.' Instead, I think of more pleasant things, like my work.

*Day of the Locust* was well received in Hollywood. I won an L.A. Drama Critics Circle award for my performance, which I took in stride: everybody loves a comeback, especially for pretty, hatchet-wielding junkies.

We did, indeed, move the show Off-Broadway where it won two Obies, one for Nigel's directing and another for me—Distinguished Performance by an Actress. I've had lots of adjectives placed in front of my name but "distinguished" was never one of them. I like it.

I drive past the cheerful "Welcome to Chowchilla" sign. With its beautiful cut-out palm trees one might expect a charming vacation getaway lies ahead instead of the largest female correction facility in the U.S. By sheer coincidence, the name "Chowchilla" translates as "murderers," according to the Native American tribe of Chaushila Yokut who settled here hundreds of years ago.

What an appropriate home for one Nikki Barnes who was fully prosecuted and convicted on two counts of first-degree murder and one count of false imprisonment. She's serving two consecutive life sentences.

Another positive thought: the cops tracked down Pierce—who actually does have a last name, Bray. And got hold of damning texts between him and Nikki. They convinced him to come clean in a plea deal and he got off with a fine and two years of community service. The fact that his father is a prominent Republican state senator may have had something to do with that. Pierce admitted to providing Nikki with not only the crack-laced joint that she placed in my purse, but also the LSD that wound up in my cranberry juice. When I'm feeling down, I conjure up the image of Pierce wearing an orange jump suit, picking up litter from the side of the 405. It always cheers me up.

I pull into the visitors parking lot and turn off the ignition. The sprawling prison buildings look grim and I can only imagine what goes on inside. In a few minutes, I'll see for myself. That's why I'm here. To see Nikki among other prisoners, slumped in a wheelchair, paralyzed from the waist down, looking vulnerable and impotent. I want this to be the last image I have of her, someone frail and harmless.

As a kid, I was always comforted by the fact that the villains in movies were always vanquished, never to return again. I would leave the theatre knowing the world was a safe place. Then my parents took me to a re-release of *Bambi*. Some off-screen hunter shot Bambi's mother and got away with it. I was convinced the bastard was still out there in the world someplace—that evil had somehow triumphed. I cried for days and had trouble sleeping at night. My dad explained it was just a movie, but I still felt unsafe. It took me weeks before I was able to sleep well again. I grab the paperwork from my purse and get out of the car.

• • •

The prison is everything you'd expect it to be. Barbed wire. Watchtowers. Guards who look as scary as the inmates. I hand over my ID and all the online paperwork I had to fill out to an unsmiling woman at the front desk of the reception room.

"You're here to see...?"

"Nikki Barnes," I say, adding, "she agreed to see me."

Why she accepted, I have no idea. It was determined we could have a contact visit, meaning I'd be allowed to sit with her in a large visiting room as opposed to a non-contact visit where the prisoner, in handcuffs, and visitor are separated by a glass partition.

I'm led to the visiting room and told to have a seat at one of the tables. I pick up a Golf Digest magazine and see it's two years old. Not that a current issue would make me want to read it.

I'm surrounded by prisoners with their husbands, boyfriends, girl-friends, parents. A couple next to me holds each other in a tight embrace, not saying a word, until a guard comes over to break them apart. "Fuck this shit," the prisoner says under her breath. There's an inmate at the end of my table who could be someone's suburban next-door-neighbor until she turns around and I see a peacock tattoo covering half her face.

I keep glancing at the double doors hoping to see Nikki being wheeled through them. I smell something awful and am horrified to find it's coming from me. There are dark, wet circles staining the underarms of my sweatshirt. I don't think I've ever smelled so bad before, even when I was held captive. My stomach is in turmoil and I need to use the bath-room but I'm afraid if I get up I'll miss Nikki. How humiliating would it be if I lost control of my bowels right here in the waiting room? I fidget in my chair, telling myself Nikki will arrive in a few minutes. No, I can't wait. I hurry to the rest room and not a second too soon.

· · ·

It's half an hour later. I've been to the rest room two more times, a bad case of diarrhea. Still no Nikki. I go up to one of the guards and ask how much longer I'll have to wait and am told to be patient, that there are other visitors ahead of me. I'm trying to decide if I need to go to the bathroom again when a female guard comes over to my table.

"I'm afraid your visit's been canceled," she says. *Oh God. Nikki's changed her mind.*

"What? Why?"

"Are you family?" she asks.

"No, I'm... I'm..." I don't know how to answer. Just a friend? I don't think so. "My name's Devon O'Keefe. I was told I—"

"Yes, I just placed your name," she says. "You look different on TV." Better, she means. Since I can't wear a wig or even a hat in here, I've strived for anonymity by going without make-up, piling my hair up into a messy bun and throwing on a "Shopping is My Cardio" sweatshirt, courtesy of Ligaya and the Out-of-the-Closet thrift shop in West Hollywood.

"I never saw that spooky program you were on, but I sure did watch that trial. Everybody here did. Not quite O.J. but right up there."

I feel my stomach churning again and fight the urge to race to the bathroom.

"Look—I don't know what's going on. When can I see Nikki? I've been waiting for over..."

"You can't see her."

"I don't understand. She agreed to see me. I filled out all those forms and flew over two thousand miles for this visit."

The guard looks to her right and left, then leans in.

"I ain't supposed to tell you," she says, her voice a hoarse whisper. "But you'll be seeing it on the news soon enough anyways."

"See what?"

"Inmate Barnes is deceased. She done took her own life." It takes a moment for this to sink in.

"Nikki killed herself? How?"

"Don't know. They ain't released that info yet."

"When did this happen?"

"'Bout half an hour ago."

• • •

I look out the airplane window at the clouds, wishing I lived in such a fluffy dreamland, high above the chaotic life below. I'm drowsy, and just as my eyelids close I see a black rose. I recall my final communiqué from Nikki, the note attached to that flower: "Lies are like stabs to the soul. They destroy you." I'm wondering if instead of accusing me of being a liar, as I initially thought, Nikki might actually be confessing. Maybe she was admitting her life was a series of tormenting lies that led to her taking her life. Her timing, though, was clearly a blatant statement, designed to unnerve me and bring me more pain. The last image I have of her, and one that will haunt me forever, is of her face pressed against mine, her eyes open but unblinking. In my mind, Nikki's with the hunter from Bambi. I can't see them, but I know they're out there.

• • •

Nikki's legacy did create something positive, something I know will help me heal. After she was arrested, the producer of her podcast asked if I'd meet with her to discuss the possibility of my replacing Nikki.

"Yeaaah, I don't think I'm quite down for that," I told her. "You want someone to dispense wisdom, get a hold of the cabbie who brought me here. He had all the answers. I got none."

"You underestimate yourself. Please—give it some thought," she said.

I did. And I realized she was right; I had something to offer. Now I talk to young people about dark things. They get me and I get them.

• • •

"I thought I might find you here." I've just stepped out of a twelve-step meeting at a church in Manhattan. I'm heading to a rehearsal for *Day of the Locust* that opens on Broadway in two weeks. I turn to see that the voice belongs to Trey. I almost don't recognize him in his wool overcoat, scarf, and cap.

"Trey! What are you doing here?"

"I listen to your radio show. You mentioned you go to morning meetings here." He cocks his head toward the church.

"No, I mean what are you doing in *New York?*"

"I go to school in Syracuse. Getting my doctorate at—you ready?" I nod, and he takes a deep breath. "The State University of New York College of Environmental Science and Forestry. Whoa! Didn't think I could do that in one breath."

I laugh. Serotonin floods my brain, improving the chemistry that's been so carefully created by Dr. Buzzelli and her bag of anti-depressants.

"Did I mention it's in Syracuse?" he asks.

"Yeah, you did kind of mention that."

"Just a train ride away."

"Right."

We stand there for a moment, until the cigarette smoke from the twelve-steppers starts wafting our way. Trey takes me by the arm and pulls me towards the curb, a gesture only people who are familiar with each other would make.

"Congratulations on the play," he says. "You must be..." He searches for the right word.

"I am. Maybe you could come down to see it?"

"Just bought my ticket." He pulls it out of the pocket of his jacket, waves it in front of my face. "Opening night. I hope they're paying you a shitload of money 'cause this bad boy cost me an arm and a leg."

"I could've gotten you a comp!"

"Nah, I believe in supporting the arts. I'll just have to eat Ramen for a few days."

I smile, realizing how much I've missed him.

"Trey... I don't even know where to begin." I tug on the scarf around my neck. "You want to walk me to rehearsal? It's not far. And we don't have to talk."

He gets the reference. He holds an imaginary key up to his lips and locks them.

We enter the flow of pedestrians on the crowded sidewalk. It's autumn and the morning is as crisp as an apple. There aren't days like this in Southern California—it's a desert. The hills of Laurel Canyon feel so far away, and I'm reminded of one more platitude: Don't judge me by my past. I don't live there anymore.

**Douglas Wood** writes, creates, and produces children's television for Disney, Warner Bros., Universal, NBC, Amazon, BBC, Netflix, and Apple. The PBS series, *Molly of Denali*, for which Wood was Story Editor received a Peabody award. Wood has also been a film executive for Steven Spielberg at Amblin Entertainment as well as several major Hollywood studios. He began his career in entertainment as an actor in Chicago where he appeared at Steppenwolf and the Goodman Theatre. He was a member of the Second City National Touring Company and the Fine Line comedy duo, which appeared at the Comedy Store and The Improv, and on *The Motown Revue with Smokey Robinson*, an NBC series for which Wood was also a writer. He lives in Topanga Canyon in the Santa Monica mountains outside of L.A. with his wife and two cats. *Ladies of the Canyon* is his first novel.

CPSIA information can be obtained
at www.ICGtesting.com
Printed in the USA
BVHW031543100920
588449BV00005B/116/J